WATCHING
JIMMY

WATCHING JIMMY

NANCY HARTRY

TUNDRA BOOKS

Published in Canada by Tundra Books,
75 Sherbourne Street, Toronto, Ontario M5A 2P9

Published in the United States by Tundra Books of Northern New York,
P.O. Box 1030, Plattsburgh, New York 12901

Library of Congress Control Number: 2008903013

Library and Archives Canada Cataloguing in Publication

Hartry, Nancy
Watching Jimmy / Nancy Hartry.

ISBN 978-0-88776-871-2

I. Title.

PS8565.A673W38 2009   jC813.'54   C2008-902093-6

We acknowledge the financial support of the Government of Canada through the
Book Publishing Industry Development Program (BPIDP) and that of the
Government of Ontario through the Ontario Media Development Corporation's
Ontario Book Initiative. We further acknowledge the support of the Canada
Council for the Arts and the Ontario Arts Council for our publishing program.

Design: Terri Nimmo

Because of Reg.

acknowledgments

Thanks to "The Group" – Susan Adach, Ann Goldring, Loris Lesynski, and Teresa Toten. *All for one and one for all.* I'd like to acknowledge my readers – Maxine and Doug Hartry, Lesley Marshall, Susan Foley, Kim Brotohusodo, Jocelyn Burke, Yvonne Thompson, and Paula Wing's class. Thanks also to Dr. Paul O'Connor for his help; to Gaelan Burke for his singing; to Marthe Jocelyn for selecting me to be part of *Secrets*; and especially to Kathryn Cole for taking such good care of Carolyn and Jimmy; and finally, to my nana, who from her perch on a cloud said, "You seem to be having trouble, dear. Just take this down."

chapter

Uncle Ted said Jimmy bumped his head falling off the swing. He said Jimmy just seemed to let go of the chains when he reached the highest arc, and he fell, *thunk*, to the ground and lay still. Uncle Ted got out of his car and ran over to Jimmy. He said he talked to him. "Jimmy. Jimmy, wake up!" He said he slapped Jimmy's face. He jiggled him. When Jimmy didn't wake up, Uncle Ted carried him to the car and placed him gently on the back-seat of his Thunderbird convertible. He didn't even stop to open up the door.

The last part is true. The getting out of the car, the talking, the jiggling, the slapping, the carrying, and even the laying down. The first part is not.

Jimmy never fell off the swing.

It was dim in the park when it happened. The street-lights had come on above the ravine, signaling the time for all the little kids to leave. It was too dusky for the lovers, and all the cigarette-puffing teenagers were at a community dance. Uncle Ted chose the perfect time to teach Jimmy a lesson he'd never forget.

Uncle Ted thought he'd get rid of any stragglers by paying them off. He snapped a blue five-dollar bill over his head, folded it lengthwise, and passed it to the horrid Luanne Price, the tallest kid. "You're the banker, my dear. Off you go, and mind the little ones don't push and shove at the Dairy Bar."

Uncle Ted just didn't count on me, Carolyn, perched in a tree where the park and the parking lot meet.

To understand the whole story, you have to go back to the evening of the last Thursday before the end of summer holidays. I know this because Uncle Ted has made it his habit to visit Aunt Jean every Thursday ever since her eldest son, Bertie, was shot down over the English Channel during the war.

Just to be perfectly clear, I call Aunt Jean *Aunt Jean* and

Uncle Ted *Uncle Ted*, but they aren't my real relatives – just close family friends who we've known forever. Uncle Ted is Aunt Jean's brother. Her only living relative, other than her youngest son, Jimmy, of course. Aunt Jean's husband has been dead since Jimmy was five. I barely remember him.

Jimmy and I were born ten days apart, and he and his mom – Aunt Jean – live in the other half of our semi-detached house, which is the end one before you go down into the park. In fact, my bedroom and Jimmy's are separated by a fire wall. When we were little, we used to do Morse Code messages on the wall after lights out, until Aunt Jean would scream "Stop that blooming racket!"

All my life, I've spent more time in Aunt Jean's house than my own, because my mom works crazy shifts at the button factory. Aunt Jean gets paid to watch me.

Like I said, on the last Thursday of the summer holidays, Uncle Ted parked in front of Aunt Jean's half of the semi. All the kids streamed out of their houses like ants to a picnic to see Uncle Ted's honey of a car; a new, baby blue-and-white Thunderbird convertible with fins like wings.

All summer long, twenty times on Thursdays, Jimmy would say to me "Yippee, it's Uncle Ted Day. Don't you

3

love that car, Carolyn? Wouldn't you love to drive that car more than anything in the world?" Every kid in the neighborhood coveted that car, but no one more than Jimmy.

Boys are so dumb about cars. I could have said "Jimmy, you need a licence to drive a car," or "Jimmy, you have to be sixteen to drive a car," but what would have been the point? I ignored him.

Every Thursday during the summer of 1958, while Uncle Ted was visiting with Aunt Jean in the back kitchen, we kids swarmed the car. We jumped on the bumper. We took little kicks at the whitewall tires. We opened the doors or slid over them and fell, *plop*, onto the white leatherette seats.

Some kids adjusted the radio or the aerial, but it was only Jimmy who sat behind the wheel. After all, Uncle Ted was his uncle so Jimmy should be the driver. Once Jimmy had slipped on Uncle Ted's white gloves, none of us asked for a turn. He wore Uncle Ted's white driving cap backwards, because otherwise, the peak blocked his vision.

"*Rummmn. Rummmmn.*" Jimmy turned an imaginary key. All the passengers ran their own engines as well. I did the running commentary, telling them what we were passing: Steeds Dairy, Bush Hardware, Armitage's Bakery – all the sights up and down King Street. We acted like a bunch of five year olds.

Jimmy got carried away at Ye Olde Candy Store and tooted the horn.

Uncle Ted burst out of Aunt Jean's house hollering. "You kids get away from my car! How many times do I have to tell you?"

The kids scuttled like cockroaches back to their houses. There was only Jimmy, Uncle Ted, and me left.

Uncle Ted shook his fist at Jimmy. "And to think I put you in charge!"

He turned to me. "How could you go along with him, Carolyn?" He handed each of us a chamois, and we spent the rest of his visiting time polishing fingerprints off that car.

"It's not much of a punishment is it, Carolyn?" Jimmy grinned so wide I thought his mouth would reach his sticky-outy ears.

I do admit, now, that I liked the polishing. When you thought you were done and looked at the paint sideways, there'd be just one more print. I liked huffing my breath on the baby blue paint and then polishing the marks away. It was a challenge.

Each week the routine was the same. When Uncle Ted left, he kissed Aunt Jean good-bye. He peeled a purple ten-dollar bill from his billfold and pressed it into her hand. We gave him back the chamois. He patted my head and punched Jimmy on the right shoulder.

Hard.

chapter

Although Uncle Ted Day was the most exciting day of the week, Fridays were a close second because we had group lessons at the community pool.

"What's that on your shoulder?" I asked Jimmy one Friday.

"Just a bruise. I must have fallen."

He couldn't fool me. That bruise on Jimmy's shoulder was an Uncle Ted Bruise. Each week it got darker and darker, one bruise on top of last week's one, on top of the one from the week before, none of them getting a chance to heal between visits.

"Uncle Ted shouldn't hit you so hard."

"He doesn't mean anything by it. I'm just a softy, that's all. And he's always swinging like a big door. He doesn't know his own strength."

I squinted my eyes at Jimmy. The last part sounded like Aunt Jean's words, the part about Ted not knowing his own strength. *Hogwash!* Uncle Ted may have been as tall and as wide as a door, but he was more like a screen door to my way of thinking. There was always hot air rushing out of him.

The Thursday before school started, the one before the long weekend, was Aunt Jean's summer wind-up Canasta tournament, but she was prepared to stay home and visit with Uncle Ted as usual.

"Go. Go. Jimmy and I will be fine," said Uncle Ted. He gave Jimmy a little love-punch on the shoulder to prove it.

Don't go, Aunt Jean, I wanted to scream. *Stay home!*

No words came out of my mouth and I deeply regret that. I deeply do.

Aunt Jean put on her white gloves. She pinned her straw hat on her head and snapped her purse shut. She kissed Jimmy good-bye. "Be good," she said, including me.

When Aunt Jean was almost out of sight, Uncle Ted turned to me, "Go home and tell your mother she wants you." I figured he wanted me to get lost so I went and sat on my porch.

"Jimmy, keep your friends away from my car." Uncle Ted took the paper and went inside.

Jimmy's friends swarmed all over the car as usual, but with Aunt Jean gone, Uncle Ted seemed more mad than usual. I think now that his anger had been building up all summer long.

When Jimmy got carried away and tooted the horn, Uncle Ted came out of the house screaming. Even I was scared, and I was not involved. Uncle Ted yanked Jimmy out of the car. He jumped in behind the wheel and started the engine.

"Get off. Get off, you kids! I'm moving this car."

He put the car in gear and went forward with a jerk. Then he slammed on the brakes. Forward, slam. Forward, slam, like a baby blue bucking bronco, until all the kids, laughing, fell off the car and onto the road. All except one.

Jimmy was splayed over the trunk holding on to an armrest in the backseat.

Uncle Ted zoomed off down the lane, into the park, with Jimmy on the trunk. All the kids followed.

I ran as fast as I could, I really did. My hair streamed off my neck and I galloped, trying to go faster.

When I got down into the park, the light was fading. The swings and the cat-poop sandbox and the picnic tables were blending in with the grass. Uncle Ted was blowing hot air about how rich and important he was and handing Luanne the five-dollar bill.

I shinnied up a tree and blended in with the leaves.

When all the kids were gone, Uncle Ted turned to Jimmy, who by this time, had jumped off the car and was standing by the driver's door. Uncle Ted punched him on his sore shoulder and then his good shoulder and then his sore shoulder.

"So you want to drive my car, do ya? Huh? Huh, you little twerp?" Jimmy kept moving back and forth during the punching and saying, "Yes, I want to drive your car!" From my perch it looked like they were doing the cha-cha dance.

Uncle Ted pushed Jimmy with two hands. "Well, you'll have to race me then."

Jimmy got on his mark, lined up with the front bumper of the car. Uncle Ted tooted the horn and they were off, Uncle Ted gunning, gunning, and Jimmy pumping his legs fast. He did pretty good. He ran straight down the parking lot. From my angle, I thought Jimmy won, but no, there had to be a re-run.

On the re-run, Uncle Ted changed the rules of the race. The car cut into Jimmy's lane. It cut him off just missing him. Jimmy kept running. When he realized that Uncle Ted was chasing him, he went even faster. Jimmy ran out onto the grass. Ted didn't care. He drove up and over the log that marked the end of the parking lot and onto the grass, carving doughnuts – trying to run Jimmy down. Jimmy darted. He deked. He leapt out of the way and dove into the backseat of the car.

I thought he was safe. But no, Jimmy was like a burr to be shaken loose. The car lurched and Jimmy was thrown from passenger door to passenger door and back again. Oh, those sore shoulders! Oh, the noise!

I started to scramble down from the tree. "Stop! Stop! Stop!" He didn't hear me.

I was dangling from the lowest branch when Jimmy's body flew out the back of the car. It arced in the air and dropped to the ground. Jimmy lay still.

The rest you know. I'm sorry I can't tell it as fast as it happened.

Apparently Uncle Ted passed Aunt Jean coming home from Canasta. Aunt Jean tells how she cradled poor Jimmy's head on the way to the hospital.

Jimmy didn't go to school on the day after Labor Day. He hasn't been to school yet, because of his head injury.

Uncle Ted still comes on Thursdays, which is fine, because Aunt Jean has no other visitors now except me, and Jimmy is a peck of trouble. A peck of trouble. Aunt Jean says that a visit from her only living relative makes a nice break. It's something to look forward to.

It is now my job to scoot the kids away from the car, which is easy, because I have a new technique.

"Can Jimmy drive your car?" I ask Uncle Ted sweetly. "His diapers won't leak a bit. They were just changed."

Uncle Ted always lets him, but I have to put down the car blanket first. Jimmy sits behind the wheel and I go, "*Rummmn. Rummmmn.*" He bounces up and down like a baby, and the other kids stay back and watch.

When it's time for Uncle Ted to leave and he is handing over a ten-dollar bill, I say, "Aunt Jean could do with some more handkerchiefs on account of Jimmy's drooling from the accident."

Uncle Ted peels off two more bills and presses them into Aunt Jean's hand. Then Uncle Ted goes to pat Jimmy on the head. Jimmy ducks. Ted tries to give me a love-punch in the shoulder. I put my two hands up like a shield and kick him in the ankle.

"Carolyn!" says Aunt Jean. I don't say anything. What would be the point?

On Monday, Tuesday, Wednesday, and Friday after school, I push Jimmy on the swings when no one's watching. He hangs on tight like he always did. He loves to go really high and touch the sky.

Our Jimmy is not scared of anything or anybody.

Neither am I.

chapter

The days are getting shorter now and Jimmy doesn't want to go down into the park. Not when he can play in the leaves and mess up my piles. Aunt Jean has asked me to rake the backyard. I didn't count on Jimmy's help.

"Stop that, Jimmy. I'll never get this done."

Jimmy lies down in the leaves, burrowing deep underneath. Then he pops up like a jack-in-the-box, wearing a hat of red and yellow maple leaves.

Jimmy can't say my name very well. His words are slurred and come out like he's snorting them through his nose. But I know what he wants. I can understand him very well. He's not a mental defective like Luanne Price said today in mathematics class, before I popped her in the nose.

Our Jimmy is in there. He really is. Sometimes I forget

about the accident because he looks exactly the same. Sometimes I go to ask him a question. Maybe, something like, "Jimmy, do you want to go down into the Humber River and ride our bikes through the leaves and see if the salmon are jumping upstream?"

Jimmy can't ride a bike because he has no balance. Even though there is nothing wrong with his legs, he walks with a gimp now, as if one leg is shorter than the other. I don't think he can remember what a salmon is. I don't think he would put it together that a jumping fish could be that pinkish, fried-in-butter delicacy that we are having for dinner tonight.

I put down my rake and play. I dive into Jimmy's pile of leaves. I toss them in the air. I chase him, throwing leaves at him, and then he chases me. When Aunt Jean calls us in, flicking the porch light on and off to save the hydro, I stop and look back. There's a tiny mound of leaves to show I tried to do something. But the rest of the yard looks like it's been stirred with a stick.

I'll get up early tomorrow and get at it before Jimmy's awake. That's what I'll do.

Aunt Jean is already "warshing" Jimmy's hands at the sink. He wants to chase the bar of soap around the bottom

of the enamel basin. Water is splashing all around and
Aunt Jean isn't laughing. She looks like she's clamping so
hard on her false teeth that they might break.

"Sit down and behave!" Aunt Jean pushes Jimmy onto a
chair. "Eat quietly. Be polite. Don't reach. Sit nice!"

I have pretty much given up scolding Jimmy like this. It
doesn't help at all because he gets frustrated. I think some
part of his poor head remembers how he used to behave
and is sad. Sad because his brain is broken.

The fish is very good, without too many bones. Aunt
Jean is more careful than she used to be about the bones
for fear of Jimmy choking. So there's *one* positive thing for
me about the new Jimmy. Just one so far. I go with Aunt
Jean and Jimmy to St. James Cathedral every Sunday, and
the dean's sermon last week was about how it's important
to find the good and the positive in everybody.

I try, Dean, but it's hard.

"I got picked to say my speech in front of the whole
school," I say, trying to distract Aunt Jean's mind from all
that Jimmy is doing wrong.

"Jimmy, use your fork. . . . Carolyn, that's wonderful.
Jimmy and I would love to come and hear your performance, wouldn't we, dear?"

Hear my performance? Jimmy? Running around the back of the auditorium, snorting and making clapping noises in all the wrong places?

"It's only for kids in the school," I say. "It's not public."

"Carolyn, we're not public. We're family."

"We'll see," I say.

Aunt Jean passes me the bowl of peas. Her eyes drill into my eyes, but I don't turn away or change my mind.

I'm practical. Jimmy can't behave, so he can't come to school. Even to hear my speech.

I lean over and catch Jimmy's tea towel before it slides onto the floor.

"There, now you're perfect," I say, tying a big knot at his neck.

"Pur-ft," Jimmy mimics, snorting like every other time he speaks.

chapter

I've told you about Jimmy's accident with the swing. I've told you about the speech I'm supposed to give at the school assembly. It's for the November 11th Remembrance Day ceremony and the topic is *Why I'm proud to be a Canadian.*

There is one thing left to tell, that is, to my way of thinking. If it was Aunt Jean talking, she would have her eyes closed by now and her lids would be fluttering and we would be off on one angle and back on another angle and you would have to figure the whole muddle out for yourself.

I'm not like that. I like to tell it straight, so when I say there's really only one thing left to fit into the puzzle, I mean it.

My mom is on regular midnight shifts, so rather than transferring me back to my own house and my own bed in the middle of the night, I've been sleeping over in Aunt Jean's spare room. My mom doesn't work Saturdays, but she went out late with the girls and didn't want to get me.

I smell a fella.

Never mind.

I laid my church clothes on the floor, exactly like an invisible person was wearing them. White gloves, white ankle socks with lace trim. Patent leather party shoes. Straw purse and hat with an elastic, so it doesn't blow away. A turquoise velvet dress with a white lace collar and a little white lace apron.

Sorry. I'm sounding like Aunt Jean. The dress has nothing to do with what happens next. That is, I don't think it does, except I do like the dress because it matches my eyes.

Maybe the dress is important after all, because when I wear it, I feel strong.

I *am* prideful.

Aunt Jean likes to go to St. James Cathedral downtown. It's some trouble to get to now with Jimmy. You have to walk a long ways and then take the King car into the city.

Jimmy is fine once we get to the streetcar. I mean, he's fine if we get a seat right up front. He likes the sound of the bell ringing and, to keep him quiet when we're in the streetcar, the driver always rings the bell way more than he should. Sometimes the driver rings the bell continuously all the way to the cathedral.

St. James Cathedral is where Aunt Jean's son Bertie, the fighter pilot with the RCAF, was buried from. Well, that was where the service was, because they never found the body. I don't think they looked too hard because the war was almost over when he was killed.

The church has big high ceilings. And flags hanging down. Some of them go way back to the War of 1812, not just the Great World Wars. There are statues and plaques on the walls with names of very important English people. I recognize some from my history books.

Once we get to St. James, the big doors are open and welcoming and the old bells are ringing. Jimmy likes the bells and we rush after him to find our seats.

Aunt Jean likes to sit up front with the ladies from Rosedale. Never mind. She lost a son and she's entitled to sit as close to God as she needs to be.

St. James has the best choir in all of Canada. The men

and boys choir sings most of the service. You really don't have to do much but pop up and down like a toilet seat. That's what the old Jimmy used to say.

Jimmy is very calm listening to the boys sing. They sound like angels. Jimmy clasps his hands in his lap and twists and twists, listening closely. It's always too soon when the altar boy carries the staff down the aisle collecting all the little lambs to go to Sunday school, but Jimmy goes off to the nursery without any trouble. He likes to follow the altar boy with the staff. I think he thinks he's in a parade.

Our Jimmy looks like such a big galoot in the nursery.

Aunt Jean lets me stay with her in the church because I love the music so much. And I can scoot out of our pew to check on Jimmy and report back to her. Aunt Jean says this is the only break she gets all week long. She'd love Sunday to go on forever.

I duck out after the offertory hymn and before the sermon. The ladies in the nursery are some glad to see me. Jimmy is in a bad way. He wants his pants off and his diapers off. I try to stop him. His hands flap me away.

So without even thinking, completely automatically, I start to sing. It's like when I open my mouth, God comes down on a beam of light, enters my brain and a sound like wind chimes comes out of my mouth.

I sing and the whole room stops, frozen by my voice. This is the one thing that I've left to tell, and if I trace things backwards, it's the thing that leads to everything else that happens. My singing voice.

Did I mention that no one except Jimmy had ever heard my voice? When the two of us used to play in the ravine, I sang for him. Just sometimes, and only for him, because he'd never tell my secret.

You probably need to know that my dad was a singer. My dad took off before I was born. Somewhere. Maybe to Vancouver. Maybe Paris, France with a floozie. We don't know. My mom and dad were married about twenty minutes before I was born. "It seemed like twenty minutes," my mom said. But those twenty minutes are an important twenty minutes, because I, Carolyn Jamieson, am not a bastard.

Aunt Jean doesn't like me to use the word *bastard*. When I say the word *bastard*, she puts her hand over her heart and gasps for air and all the time her eyelids flutter like mad. She calls it *illegitimate* but I know it means the same thing. Although, the usage is tricky. *A* bastard, an illegitimate child, is different from *the* bastard, a man who marries his wife and takes off after twenty minutes.

You might like to know that Luanne Price and I were friends once, a long time ago, in Grade 2. She is never just Luanne Price. Now, I call her the *horrid* Luanne Price. To her face. Back in Grade 2, I went to her house to play, although she was never allowed to come to mine, because my mother worked, she said. Because we needed more supervision, she said.

I didn't care why I was invited to play. Luanne Price is an only child and she had books that came all the way from England. I see now that her mother only wanted me to play with Luanne because I could read and she wanted her precious baby to catch the reading bug. I would read out loud to Luanne while she played with her dolls. Then Luanne would try and sound out the words. Sometimes we put on plays, acting out the stories. It was wonderful until one cloudy day, the horrid Luanne Price and I played house in her backyard. She wanted to know where my daddy was. Or if I even had a daddy, at all. She wanted to see a picture of him. Did I keep a picture of him in the locket I wore around my neck, because she'd heard her daddy say that I was a "poor little bastard."

Me, a bastard!

I was so mad, I could have spit. Imagine. Me, a bastard! The worst name you could be called. A name that would be branded on your birth certificate to follow you around for the rest of your natural-born days.

I put Luanne Price in a headlock. I did not, and do not, pull hair. Pulling hair is girl fighting. I fought like Jimmy taught me. I twisted her little chicken arm behind her back and dragged her up the stairs to the bathroom. The radio was blaring in the kitchen and Luanne's mom was singing while making supper. She was singing along with Frank Sinatra who was *Singing in the Rain.* I remember that especially, because it was raining outside.

Luanne's mother uses Camay. The bar is pink and matches the pink and black tiles in the bathroom. I remember this particularly, because I wondered if pink soap tasted better than white soap.

"You wouldn't dare!" Luanne's eyes bugged out of her head.

"Mom! Mom!" But I'd kicked the door closed. I ran the water. I wet the pink bar of soap.

"Bite it!"

Luanne kicked and struggled. It was all I could do to keep her in a headlock.

"Bite it. Open your mouth." She knew I wouldn't let her go. When she opened her mouth to scream, I shoved the bar into it.

"Take, it back, Luanne. You take it back." I was very calm. When she started to gag, I let her go.

The bar of soap fell from Luanne's mouth, onto the floor. In her hands she cupped water from the tap and took a gulp. With one hand, then the other hand, she wiped her face and spit in the sink. She looked like she was going to bring up.

I never played with the horrid Luanne Price again. I have no use for Luanne Price, or her father or anybody else in that family, and when her mother phoned mine to complain about my behavior, I refused to apologize. I will never forget the look on my mother's face when I told her what happened. She did not actually faint, but I thought she might. Well. She gave Mrs. Price a piece of her mind and hung up smartly.

Never mind. They are all nosy parkers in that family. Now, Luanne vies with me for top marks in class. But she can't hurt me, because I don't care all that much about school. But music, that's a different thing altogether.

So, you can only imagine how badly Jimmy was behaving for me to sing like *the* bastard.

The nursery lady comes up to me and takes my face between her hands.

"Oh, Carolyn. You have a God-given gift. You must use it."

I pull away and start putting Jimmy's socks back on.

"No dear, I insist. You must sing in a choir. Pity you're not a boy."

I toss my braids. She must be able to read my mind. I've been praying so hard to be transformed into a boy but it never, ever happens.

"There's a wonderful choir at St. Olave's. Right in your neighborhood. I'll make enquiries although auditions were over long ago. I'm sure they will make an exception. You are exceptional, dear."

"I don't think so," I say.

She runs on without listening to me. "There's only one practice, Thursday evening . . ."

"Did you say Thursday?"

"Of course, Thursday. Thursday is choir night in Canada." She smiles at her own little joke.

"I can't go on Ted-day."

"Pardon, dear?"

"I'm busy on Thursdays. I have important responsibilities on Thursdays. I never go out on Thursdays."

The nursery lady purses her lips in a line. "We'll see."

I turn back to Jimmy who's sitting on the floor and tug on his arms. "We'll see. We'll saw. We'll see. We'll saw."

Jimmy starts to giggle and I join in. The notion of me going to choir on Thursday is just about the craziest thing I've heard, since the Thursday before Labor Day.

27

chapter

5

Aunt Jean asked me to come home directly after
school. *Do Not Pass Go. Do Not Collect $200.* She has to
run up to Bloor Street to the bank. She has an appoint-
ment with the bank manager.

I don't mind. Mom is working an extra shift and there's
no one out on the street to play with because the days are
getting so short now.

I'm supposed to watch Jimmy while Aunt Jean is gone.
Sometimes that's very hard to do, depending on whether
he's having a good day or a bad day. When I come in the
front door, I can tell it's been a so-so day. Aunt Jean has
managed to do some things like the laundry and the dishes.
The potatoes aren't peeled. So, I help. I sit at the kitchen
table with a pot of water filled with muddy potatoes from

the garden. I select a paring knife that I test with my thumb. Aunt Jean keeps her knives very sharp, because you are more likely to cut yourself with a dull knife than a sharp one.

Jimmy swipes at me, wanting the knife.

"No, Jimmy." I try to distract him with a rag doll.

He lunges at me again. He's bigger than me. Two times as big as me, but I'm quick and wiry.

I put the potatoes and the knife on the counter, well back. Together, Jimmy and I cover the table with newspaper. I carve a star in one of the potatoes and dilute a bit of food coloring in water and pour it in a pie plate.

Jimmy stamps the star all over the paper, letting me finally get at the potato peeling.

"Stay on the paper, Jimmy. You're making a mess."

I hum a tune and Jimmy stops to listen. This is New-Jimmy behavior. I mean, he liked my singing before, but it never captivated him like it does now. It really didn't.

I won't tell my mom that I'm watching Jimmy for Aunt Jean. Aunt Jean is paid to watch me, not me to watch Jimmy. Since the troubles, I know my mom has paid Aunt Jean more wages. Half again what she used to pay. It's expensive to take the streetcar downtown to see the doctors at Sick Children's Hospital. The doctors who looked at Jimmy are all specialists. They think he has terrible headaches but because he can't talk, they can't tell for sure. They poked and prodded and X-rayed Jimmy's poor little brain, but other than that, Aunt Jean says they don't seem to know what to do.

Except Dr. Phillips. He has a plan. He thinks there is pressure on Jimmy's brain. Jimmy has a bruise on the brain and Dr. Phillips thinks he could relieve it by drilling a hole in Jimmy's head and sucking out the blood like a vampire.

I've noticed something about troubles. When Jimmy first "fell off the swing" and he was lying in a coma, his house was filled with ham and scalloped potatoes. There were Empire cookies and date squares. Cold roast beef and coleslaw. There was so much food that it spilled over into our side of the semi-detached house, because my mom has a refrigerator that my grandfather bought before he died. Aunt Jean is still using an old-fashioned icebox and it's not that easy to get ice anymore. The food lasted for two weeks. I mean, the delivery of the food, and then it stopped. Just like that. It didn't dwindle down to one canasta lady bringing one thing, and another coming forward a few days later. I mean, it just stalled out at the two-week mark, like two weeks was sufficient time for us to get used to the new Jimmy.

Well, it wasn't.

I heard my mom and Aunt Jean talking over their teacups while I was supposed to be memorizing my spelling list. An operation for Jimmy will be very expensive. Aunt Jean will have to mortgage the house. She's gone up to Bloor Street to sign the papers and the scent of Chanel No. 5 that she dabbed behind her ears to impress the bank manager remains in the house.

I'm not stupid. If you mortgage a house, you get money from the Bank, but you have to pay it back. If you don't pay it back, you can lose your home and be on the street with your suitcases. Aunt Jean is always reminding us what it was like in the Great Depression. The war didn't hold a candle to the Great Depression, except that Bertie died. And Aunt Jean has had to sell so many of her grandmother's things and her wedding gifts. You might think my mom and I are fairly well set in comparison, because my grandpa left us his house with all the stuff in it, including a piano. But we're not. There are expenses, real expenses for heating oil and food. We stopped my piano lessons shortly after Grandpa died. Like Aunt Jean, we just get by now.

Jimmy likes show tunes. And big band tunes. He's partial to Glen Miller. I turn the radio up when he's on, but even so, it's not as calming for Jimmy as my voice singing Glen Miller. I hand Jimmy a wooden spoon. He beats the table and keeps pretty good time. I sing into a whisk. We make such a racket that we don't hear Aunt Jean come in. She's been standing watching us for some time, I think. Me singing and Jimmy beating on the drum.

Aunt Jean's face is pale. Bits of hair, gray and brown, straggle out of her bun. She's twisting her hands like Jimmy does when he's agitated.

"Mercy, Aunt Jean, you look like you've seen a ghost. Sit down." I push a kitchen chair toward her. I run some tap water and hand her a glass.

I'm afraid to ask the question, but I need to know. "Did the bank manager say no? Can't you get a mortgage?"

Aunt Jean takes a tiny sip and closes her eyes. The lids are fluttering. It's going to be a long one.

"Aunt Jean. Tell me." I try to sound bossy. "Now."

"There's already a mortgage."

"What? I don't understand."

"Neither did I. Apparently, Ted holds a mortgage. The bank did a search at the Registry Office and there's already a mortgage in Ted's name. The bank won't give me any money."

"But this is your house!"

"Three years before my Jake died, he needed money and borrowed some from Ted. Ted registered a mortgage."

"And Jake never told you?"

"Never. I haven't paid back a red cent to Ted. He never asked me to."

I take the potatoes to the sink and dump them in. I wash all the garden dirt down the drain. I'm buying time.

I turn around and face Aunt Jean. "It's simple. Tell him to forget the loan. Tell him to make you a gift."

Aunt Jean straightens her shoulders. "I already did. Ted has another solution. He wants to move out of his apartment and into your room upstairs. I called him from the bank."

"Oh, no!"

"Ted says I can't afford to pay him back so the house is as good as his."

Jimmy gives the wooden spoon a mighty *swack*. The handle splinters and breaks in his hand.

Jimmy snorts and wails. I want to wail, too, but I'm far too grown up.

chapter

6

Aunt Jean is very determined to get to St. James Cathedral early, well before the 11:00 service begins. She needs to pray. She needs to pray very badly.

I let Jimmy run outside on the lawn. The church is magnificent with tall trees reaching up to heaven. Some of the shrubbery is red, like the burning bush in the Bible. There's a carpet of yellow maple leaves for Jimmy to slide on. I chase him, he chases me. Jimmy's cheeks are pink like crisp McIntosh apples.

There are strangers hanging about. Men, grizzled and sleepy, smelling of drink. One of them is raving about the war. It's like the fellow knew Bertie, but of course, that's impossible. He's talking about war heroes and all the medals they would have got if only they weren't shot down in flames. Listening to him, you can almost imagine Bertie's plane exploding and raining fire over the English Channel until he just sizzled right out.

I stand between the man and Jimmy, protecting him. If Aunt Jean were here, she'd yank Jimmy away. Aunt Jean is a Temperance Leaguer and can't abide drink. Before Jimmy "fell off the swing," she used to march to keep our neighborhood closed to taverns. It's a source of great pride to her that our neighborhood is still dry.

Did I mention Jake, Jimmy's dad, died from drink? He wasn't a mean drunk, but he couldn't keep a job, not even during the war when able men dwindled down to nothing, which is why he needed to work for himself. Aunt Jean said it was God's will that her oldest son, Bertie, got her husband's feet instead of her own. Jimmy got his mother's flat feet too, but never mind, if there was a war tomorrow, they'd never take Jimmy, feet or no feet. Jimmy is far too addle-brained.

The soldier is telling Jimmy about how the church property is really a cemetery. Underneath the green sod are masses of bones from a cholera epidemic. Bones of children and old people, mothers and fathers, just shoveled into a mass grave like the Jews and the Poles and the gypsies were shoveled into pits in Europe.

"Come on, Jimmy." But Jimmy won't leave. Finally, the man takes Jimmy's hand and walks him to the church steps. The church bells are ringing now, and Jimmy is anxious to get inside. He tugs the man up the steps.

"Sorry, son," he says. "I have renounced the Lord. I'll not enter his house after everything I've seen."

Jimmy takes off on his own and runs into the church.

"Do you live in the streets?" I ask. The man looks dirty and poor, but he talks sensibly, like a teacher.

"I'm a citizen of the world. I live where I can."

I give him an apple I'd been saving for Jimmy. The man palms the apple like I've given him the keys to Uncle Ted's car.

I find Jimmy with Aunt Jean. The men and boys choir is just finishing up their rehearsal, singing a motet in old English. Their voices move like waves on a beach, up and down the scale, tone by tone. The final note of the organ is suspended in the air and I feel like I can reach right out and grab it.

The Rosedale ladies are filing in. Some in black, all in flouncy hats. I like sitting at the front of the church smelling the face powder and the different perfumes. It's like sitting in Aunt Jean's garden in the summer.

Usually we have lots of room in our pew – we usually have it to ourselves. If someone opens the door and sits in our box by mistake, once they get a whiff of Jimmy's urine smell, they usually find a reason to move elsewhere – a friend they need to see across the aisle, a sidesman they need to chat with. The Rosedale ladies are polite or try to be. Aunt Jean says that they have good breeding. Like her hybrid tea roses, I guess.

There is only one person in the whole congregation who doesn't care about Jimmy's smell. The General. I don't even know his last name. Aunt Jean and I just call him the General. Perhaps his nose has been blunted by nerve gases and gunpowder and he can no longer smell. The General sits right beside the door of our box so he can get out quickly to read the lesson. Since he retired from his post in Germany, the General reads the lesson every week. He's a regular feature.

I like to look at the General's face. He has young skin, smooth and pink. His eyes are bright like a baby's, darting around looking at everyone. His most shocking feature is his white hair. It's as white as the dean's surplice, and sticks straight up like the bristles on a shoeshine brush. They say he was in Europe two weeks and after a day of fighting, he went to bed with black hair and when he woke up in the morning, his hair had turned completely white. As if the color was scared right out of it!

When the General gets up to read, people shift in their seats and lean forward. A murmur goes through the crowd. The General is a true hero. He has things to say, and he never sticks to his notes.

Aunt Jean pokes me in the ribs. It's time to check on Jimmy. I pull my arm in tight and ignore her. I want so badly to stay and listen. Every week, the General wanders into war.

"Carolyn!" Aunt Jean's annoyed.

I sigh loudly, dramatically, so they can hear me right up to the front of the church, but I go. I dawdle all the way to the nursery, punishing Aunt Jean. Punishing my mother for working all the time so that I have to come to church with Aunt Jean. Sunday is supposed to be a day of rest, but my mother never rests. And yes, punishing the new Jimmy.

Did I mention my mother was out again last night? There must be a fella that she's keeping from me. She probably doesn't want me to frighten him away. The last time I actually met one, I pretended I was a dog with distemper, frothing at the mouth and baring my fangs in his face. He couldn't get out the door fast enough. I don't get to see much of my mother as it is. We don't need outsiders.

I find the choir room. There are rows of benches facing each other with a piano in the middle. The sheet music is everywhere – on the floor, on the benches. Boys can be so careless. I pick the papers up off the floor and pile them neatly on the piano. Then I sit down on the piano bench. I finger the first line of a Gregorian chant without depressing the keys for fear that the congregation might hear me. I play to the end and start again, humming now. I go back to the beginning and sing softly. Then I change key and sing the chant that is running through my head.

There are always new tunes in my head and I have to, HAVE TO, let them fall on the page or they will drive me around the bend all day long. I keep one dictation book between the mattress and boxspring at home and a similar one at Aunt Jean's, since the music flows best first thing in the morning, before I'm truly awake. There was no time for writing down my music this morning.

I open my eyes and the General is standing before me.

He's holding the hand of a towheaded toddler, peeking out at me from behind his Grandpa's leg.

"This is Armstrong."

"Hi ya, Armstrong." I ask the General if he wants me to take the kid to the nursery.

"Please. Maybe he'll mind you. I'm not having much luck."

I take Armstrong's other hand and we swing him up some stairs and down the hall. Armstrong wants to go by himself and he runs toward the brightly lit room.

"My daughter-in-law is supervising the nursery. He doesn't like to share his mother with the other children so he makes a fuss."

"He'll learn," I say. "There's no point in making a fuss."

Jimmy's glad to see me. I reintroduce him to the General who has met us just once before. He shakes Jimmy's hand and calls him "young man."

"What happened?" the General asks and I know exactly what he means. I've told the story about the swing so many times, even I almost believe it happened that way. I tell it again.

There is a long pause while the General waits for me to add more. There is nothing left to say.

"I don't like the sound of that, young lady. A big strapping boy, falling off a swing. There's something not quite right with that tale." His bright blue eyes scour my face, looking for the truth. I turn away first.

The General's daughter-in-law, the nursery lady, wants me to sing. I begin to protest and then figure singing might divert the General from asking further questions leading to Uncle Ted, Aunt Jean's only living relative – such as he is.

I sing the "White Cliffs of Dover." It's a war song, not a church song. I can see by the look on the General's face that he's no longer in the nursery at St. James Cathedral in Toronto, but back in Europe, during war time.

I don't end it, the song, I mean. I make a key change and switch into "Jesus Loves Me."

One thing I know for sure. Jesus doesn't love Jimmy or Aunt Jean. He must really be mad at them for something. As Aunt Jean says, things go from bad to worse. I would say to *worser*, which I know is not a word, but it says how I feel.

Things go from bad to worse to worser. Worser and worser.

chapter

There are many whispering conversations at Aunt Jean's kitchen table that I'm excluded from. Little pitchers have big ears.

I squirm on my stomach and hide under the end table in the parlor, being careful not to move the lamp cord, but positioning myself close enough to hear. Mom and Aunt Jean are talking about money. Where was Aunt Jean going to get the money to pay back Uncle Ted? He was being so insistent about being paid off. My mom offers to put a mortgage on our house and give it to Aunt Jean.

"I can't ask you to do that, dear. It's not right. You have troubles of your own."

That means me. My mom jokes that I'm "boilin' trouble," just like the nursery rhyme. I love the way her nose crinkles and her eyes smile when she says it.

The phone rings. It's the General's daughter-in-law from St. James Cathedral. She wants to speak to me.

Did I mention that I don't like the telephone? When you use the telephone, you can't see the expression in the other person's eyes. You can't match the words they're saying out of their mouths with the truth they're telling from the "windows of their soul" as the dean would put it. I have to listen very hard when I use the telephone. I try to use X-ray vision and imagine the person at the other end of the curly black wire.

"Tell her I'm not home," I pipe up from my hiding place under the end table.

"Land sakes! Get out of there, girl," says Aunt Jean.

"Carolyn, I taught you to have better manners than that. Answer the telephone," Mom says.

The black snake is curled up on the telephone table. I hesitate before picking up the receiver. "Hello?"

The General's daughter-in-law is calling on behalf of the General. The General has arranged for me to audition with St. Olave's Choir. Never mind that time for auditioning is over. They are doing their Christmas repertoire now, and they need a good soloist.

"I'm too busy at school," I say.

The General's daughter-in-law is very persuasive. It's a great honor to be invited.

"I don't go out after school," I say. I turn my back on my mother and Aunt Jean so they can't hear me. "I look after Jimmy."

"The General said to tell you it pays money."

There's a long silence. Money? I could get a job? Me, an eleven-almost twelve-year-old kid could get a job?

"I'm not interested," I say.

"He says ten dollars a week."

I'm breathing hard into the phone. My mother works one whole day in the factory for ten dollars.

"And if you do a solo, there's more."

"How much?" I whisper.

"Another ten dollars."

I don't say anything.

"Write this down." It's an order from the General's daughter-in-law. I pick up a pencil and do what I'm told. St. Olave's is within walking distance, on Windermere Avenue, close to Bloor Street. Maybe it's meant to be.

"So, can I tell them you'll be there?"

"When is it?"

"Tomorrow. Thursday."

"Oh," I say. "I never go out on Ted-day." I hang up the phone gently without saying good-bye. I fold over the paper and shove it in the pocket of my sweater coat.

When I go back to the kitchen, Jimmy is sitting in Aunt Jean's lap, facing her. He's counting her eyes and her nose and her mouth. The kitchen is warm and light, and the smell of cinnamon-baked apples is coming from the oven. The two of them are laughing.

There will be no laughing if Uncle Ted moves in.

"What did the lady want?" my mother asks.

"She wants me to help her in the nursery." The lie comes easily.

"That's a nice thing to do. It's good experience."

"It's God's work," says Aunt Jean.

Yes. Yes it is. But God is a cheapskate. Working in the nursery won't pay down the mortgage. And I don't need the Bible to tell me that there will be no smells of cinnamon coming from this kitchen if Aunt Jean and Jimmy's bags are on the street. I don't for a minute think that Aunt Jean will let Ted take over her house. She'd leave before that happened.

This I know.

chapter

I wake up with a sour feeling in my stomach. Today is Ted-day. And the day of the audition.

It's quiet on our side of the house because my mom has already left for work – the day shift this time. I listen for noise on the other side of the wall. It's like I have X-ray eyes. I can see Jimmy still sleeping, clutching his rag doll and Aunt Jean already in the kitchen, scuffing in her slippers between the kettle and the icebox, making tea and oatmeal porridge – something to stick to my ribs, because it's getting cold outside. She'll be taking down a jar of home-preserved applesauce to heat on the stove for me. Aunt Jean says that I'm getting so grown up that there's not much she can do for me now except make me a hearty breakfast and send me on my way to school. At almost twelve, I'm getting that big.

I use the bathroom and brush my teeth, pondering what I'll wear. It's going to be a mixed day today. I need a little bit of courage.

I select my navy box-pleated skirt and matching kneesocks. The white blouse with the ruffle at the sleeve. And a red cardigan. Lambswool, soft as a baby's bum, handed down from my second cousin in Montreal.

I brush my hair fifteen strokes. That will have to do.

I'm careful to check that the stove is off, that the refrigerator door is closed, that all the lights are out. I check the back door and lock the front.

I time it just perfectly. Aunt Jean is pouring me a cup of Kid's Tea.

"Good morning, dear," she says. "You look nice. Do you have to do your speech today?"

"Maybe." I don't want to deal with any suggestion that Jimmy might want to come and hear me.

"Well, you look lovely. Ready for anything the day might bring."

I observe Aunt Jean closely. There are little gray hairs sprouting from her chin. Without rouge and face powder, her cheeks are sallow and there is a crust of sleeplessness in the corner of each eye. I don't need to ask how she slept. It's written all over her face.

Aunt Jean hugs her teacup with both hands. They're beautiful hands – strong hands with well-buffed nails cut short. Her hands are in water so much that she plasters them with Nivea and wears cotton gloves to bed. She's always remarking that it's important to have lady-like hands when you get older. It's your hands that are a true giveaway of your age.

Aunt Jean's age is a mystery to me. Sometimes she seems so old, more like a grandmother to Jimmy than a mother. I mean, there was a big gap between Jimmy and Bertie. Jimmy was born after Bertie died so close to the end of the war. Jimmy never, ever met his big brother. Aunt Jean says that Jimmy-boy saved her life, or at least from a trip to the 999 Queen Street mental institution. One thing I can tell you, we never ride the Queen car – only the King car – so as to avoid passing by 999 Queen. There are many loonies still in there because of the war. The Queen car brings back bad memories for Aunt Jean because the doctors wanted to put her in there for a while, but she refused to go, and pulled out of it on her own. Mostly because of Jimmy.

Aunt Jean makes her porridge with milk. There's a dollop of butter melting on the top. With a bit of cream, it's a delicious breakfast and it's gone in a second. The applesauce is tart. I swish it around in my mouth, cleaning my teeth.

"Ted called last night. He has to take the car in today for servicing so he won't be over tonight."

He could take the bus, I think to myself. I know how Aunt Jean counts on the money he brings, but for Jimmy's sake, I'm glad. Jimmy will be better without the visit.

Did I say that Jimmy is always wilder when Uncle Ted is around? Last week, he flung his milk across the table and ruined Ted's new pants. Jimmy does the things that I think about doing. Sometimes, I give him a brain message. *Jimmy, pick up your chocolate milk and throw it at Ted.* And Jimmy does it.

Scary.

Our Jimmy's brain works on a different level now. A level most people know nothing about. He's like an animal surviving on instinct.

"So, did you talk to your brother about the mortgage?" I make a point of not calling Ted by name.

"Not another word!" she says pounding her palm on

the table. Then she softens her tone with me. "There's no talking to Ted right now. He's got a bee in his bonnet about moving into this house."

"So, Aunt Jean, you'll be home this evening, then. You won't be going out?"

Aunt Jean gives me an exasperated look like *Where else would I be going?*

"Do you have something on after school, Carolyn?"

"I think I have a speech practice, but that's after dinner." I'm glad I'm not the one matching what is coming out of my mouth with the look in my eyes, for I'm lying again. I'm setting the stage in case I decide to go to the audition, after all. I didn't say I wouldn't, so maybe I will. We'll see. It will depend on how the day goes.

I'll look for signs that I should go to the audition.

The first positive sign is that the horrid Luanne Price isn't in school today. Her teacher's-pet seat, right up front, is empty and the teacher is using it to dispense the seat work. It's a very good use of Luanne's desk to my way of thinking.

You're probably wondering what kind of student I am. These days, I'm a very inattentive student. I keep to myself mostly and I read books. I ignore the silly games that the boys play, like flicking spitballs. I pretend I don't see the regular flow of silly girlie notes moving up and down the aisles all around me, avoiding me. Since Jimmy's accident, I have cooties. Even the teachers treat me differently.

My revenge is that I never listen or never appear to listen, but I *always* know the answer to the teacher's questions. The teacher calls me, trying to catch me up, but she never can. Since the beginning of the school year, it feels like the teacher is always trying to trip me up. She makes a mission of trying to trip me up. By the third week, she leaves me alone. I wear her down.

All my marks are A+. I don't bother about school, really. I used to love, love, love it, but since Jimmy's accident ... well ... it doesn't seem very important. Now, I put in time. I do the homework. And that's it. They don't own my brain. I couldn't care less.

Right now, I'm reading *Jane Eyre*. I believe I'm reincarnated from Georgian times. Next, I'll be reading *Wuthering Heights*. I'll have to go to the adult section of the Runnymede Library and say that I'm taking it out for Aunt Jean. The Librarian thinks that Aunt Jean is quite a reader, but maybe not. She told me that Aunt Jean will have to come in herself if she intends to read *Madame Bovary*. She couldn't entrust that one to the hands of an innocent minor like me.

The second sign is shocking, really. The record player in the office is broken and there's no "God Save the Queen" today. Every morning, I work very hard at not belting out that song, because I love it so. I imagine how Jane Eyre must have sung it. So proud. So strong. With such a lovely English accent. I can't remember a weekday without "God Save the Queen."

I pass through lunch and recess and gym class thinking that that's it. There'll be no third sign and I won't have to go to the audition, after all. I can go home and do my homework and have dinner as usual and maybe play some Scrabble with Aunt Jean before bed. I almost convince myself that a boring evening would make for a very good Ted-day for a change.

I watch the clock as it passes 3:30. There are twenty minutes left until I can pack up my books.

There's a commotion at the door. The principal is smiling at me and curling his pointer finger beckoning me out of the class. *Come here, my pretty!* he seems to say, just like in the *Wizard of OZ*.

The principal has an envelope for me to take home to Aunt Jean. Expressing his congratulations. And to Jimmy, of course, who is technically still enrolled as a student, although he can't attend.

"Your Aunt Jean has been chosen as the Silver Cross Mother. Isn't that grand?"

I stare at the principal for a long time and he doesn't blink away from me. I'm reduced to asking. "How do you know?"

He purses his skinny lips and smirks. "Does Eaton's tell Simpson's, my dear? I just know. I was in the war and I still have friends in high places."

He means it. Aunt Jean is a Silver Cross Mother – chosen especially to represent all the mothers in Ontario who have lost sons in battle.

Wow. That clinches it. I'm going to the audition tonight. It's God's will.

chapter

9

And so it must be God's will that, as I'm coming up our street, I see a blue-and-white Thunderbird convertible parked in front of the house.

Pooh, it's a mirage. A *mirage* is something we're talking about in science, so my brain's decided to paint a phony picture of my worst fears for me.

It's a mirage. It's a mirage. It's a mirage.

I want so much for that car to be a mirage, I reach out and touch a blue fin before I believe it's not. My hand flies back as if I've touched a hot iron pan.

"Bastard."

I think about just going home. *Go home, you silly goose. Find your own roost.* But I don't listen to myself. I'm like a sleepwalker now, opening up Aunt Jean's front door, taking off my coat, hanging it up, lining up my galoshes underneath.

"Aunt Jean," I call. "Aunt Jean?" I wait and listen.

No answer.

Where is she? There's no one in the kitchen. There's a half-played game of solitaire laid out on the table, so Aunt Jean can't have been expecting a visitor. I notice she has three easy moves and I reach to make them for her, but then I remember that I've more important things to do. My brain is diverting me.

"Jimmy? Aunt Jean?"

I walk into the parlor. Not in all my days would I have expected to see what I see.

Jimmy and Ted are sitting on the chesterfield, close together like glue. Jimmy is quiet. For once. Aunt Jean is nowhere to be seen.

On the table is a bottle of whiskey. The cap is off and it's two-thirds empty. Uncle Ted is holding a glass. Jimmy's holding a glass.

Jimmy has been drinking rye whiskey with Uncle Ted!

I put my hands on my hips. "And what is going on in here?" I say, mimicking Aunt Jean.

Ted and Jimmy look up at me. Jimmy smiles a welcome smile that's now more crooked than ever. Ted says nothing.

"Where's Aunt Jean?"

"Where's Aunt Jean. Where's Aunt Jean. You sound like a fishwife, Carolyn. Me and Jimmy-boy were just having some fun, weren't we Jimmy? He was driving me nuts, tearing around the place, so I gave him a sip to settle him down. What's wrong with that?"

"Everything is wrong with that. You could hurt him ..." The words *more than you already have* hover, unspoken, in the air between us.

Ted narrows his slitty little snake eyes. He takes me in as if he's seeing me for the very first time from my socks, to my ankles, to my knees, up to my box-pleated skirt. I have the feeling he wants to look under that skirt.

No one – NO ONE – has ever looked at me like that. I've seen men look at my mom that way, but she has bosoms. I don't.

"Jimmy, put that down!"

He starts to drink faster and begins to choke. Whisky is spraying out of his nose and his mouth and all over the living-room rug.

Ted leans over and clips Jimmy on the side of his head.

"You leave his poor head alone! Haven't you done enough to his poor head?"

Like a rattlesnake, Ted grabs my wrist and tugs me forward. I stumble into his lap. The bottle teeters on the coffee table and crashes, spilling rye on Aunt Jean's lace doilies.

"Now you've done it!" Ted shouts.

His breath smells like gasoline. The whole room smells like gasoline. I'd be afraid to light a match for fear that the room would blow up. I'm so surprised, that I'm thinking stupid and unimportant things in slow motion. *Wake up. Wake up.*

"Let me go!" I tug my arm.

"Let's kiss and make up," says Uncle Ted.

My heart stops.

My brain does not.

I pretend to struggle. I pretend to give in. I offer my cheek to him. Then, like a vampire, I bite him on the neck. I'm like a mad dog and I won't let go.

I knee him in the groin. I have strong pointy kneecaps like spears.

Uncle Ted is holding his neck. I've drawn blood. He

drops to the floor on his knees. He looks like he's praying except his hands are now clutching his man parts.

I yank Jimmy off the couch and run him to the kitchen. He smells like a still and his diaper hasn't been changed. I can hear Uncle Ted scrabbling around, trying to get up.

"Hurry, Jimmy!"

I grab his coat and my coat as I run by the hooks in the hall. There's no time for boots. I slip my feet into Aunt Jean's shoes. Jimmy will have to make do with his slippers.

What to do? What to do? Ted knows where the key is to my house. That will be the first place he'll look.

"Run, Jimmy. Run!"

We're running up Windermere Avenue, running, and me with no good idea where to go. Where's Aunt Jean? Why would she leave?

We're almost at Bloor Street now. Jimmy's slippers are flopping through puddles, sliding on leaves. I have to hold onto him so tight.

Maybe she's in the bank. I peek in the window. The lights are out. There's no one there.

My mom is working a double shift today. She won't be home until after midnight!

Jimmy and I have nowhere to go.

"Come on, Jimmy."

We double back and I slip into St. Olave's Church basement. I've never darkened the door of the place. Ted will never find us here. And I need a place to think.

"May I help you?" the caretaker says.

"*O-ooph.* You scared me. Yes. Please."

"Do you have business with the Church?" He's leaning on the broom. His nose is wrinkling with the smell of Jimmy's diaper and the rye whiskey. It's a breathtaking combination.

My lungs are heaving. My mind is racing. And then it stops. I take a big gulp of air and in my best elocution voice, I say, "We're here for the audition."

chapter

The caretaker hustles us to the minister's office. The minister is sitting at his desk doing paperwork. We've surprised him, but he does very well at trying not to be repulsed by us, by Jimmy's stench, and my fly-away look. He shakes Jimmy's hand first and then mine and introduces himself as Mr. MacGregor. He reminds me of my grandpa.

"We've . . . I've come for the audition. This is my friend Jimmy. I'm babysitting him."

"And who are you?"

"Carolyn . . ."

"Are you members of the Church?"

"Oh, no. We go to St. James downtown, but the General called to see if it would be okay for me to try out for the choir."

The minister clears his throat and drums his fingers on the desk. "Well, Carolyn, you're awfully early. Have you had your supper yet?"

"Did Ted . . . did you have supper, Jimmy?"

Jimmy sways and snorts and cracks a crooked smile. He's drunk and he's not answering.

"Well, sir, I didn't." All of a sudden I'm tired and overcome. I sit down in a plush chair with a plunk.

The minister picks up the phone and makes a quiet call. He gathers up his papers and stuffs them in his briefcase.

"It's my sermon for Sunday. It's not very good."

He has a nice smile. I want to tell him the whole story. I want to seize the phone and call home. It's not at all like Aunt Jean to be out at this time of day. Something dreadful has happened, I know it.

"Maybe I could help you." I think I probably could. The minister doesn't know that I'm good at making up speeches or that I've won all the public speaking championships for the last three years. I won't tell him because it would sound boastful and boasting is probably a sin right up there with coveting your neighbor's house – and his ass. But it's the truth.

The minister laughs. "You already have. Carolyn. Do you and Jimmy have last names?"

"Jimmy! Put on your slippers! You can't walk barefoot outside!" I deflect the minister's question about our names.

Mr. MacGregor takes us through the church, out into the garden and down the street to the rectory. When he opens the door, the smell is heavenly, like roast chicken and apple combined. Suddenly, I'm hungry.

The minister introduces us to Mrs. MacGregor who is all bosom and looks like she's had about twenty children. She takes us into the bathroom where I wash my hands and face and comb my hair with a lavender-scented brush. She draws a bath and, when Jimmy sees the bubbles in the tub, he's eager to get in and play. He's happy to stay with Mrs. MacGregor.

"Could you rinse me out a glass, dear?" She opens up a medicine cabinet and takes out a Bromo Seltzer tablet and puts it in the bottom of the glass.

I would never have thought of that. Bromo Seltzer!

"Hey, Jimmy. Look at this. You can drink the bubbles, but you have to do it really quick before they disappear!" I say.

Jimmy swipes the glass out of my hand and opens his throat and pours it in.

"*Bleckh.*" Jimmy wipes his mouth with the back of his hand and grins at us crazily.

"We'll be fine, now, won't we, dear?"

I barely close the door behind me when I hear Jimmy vomiting. I can feel my stomach rise up my throat and I begin to gag, too. Poor Jimmy. He hates sick-up.

"That's a boy, Jimmy. Look what you've done now! The bubbles are in the toilet. Are you all finished now? Time for a bath?" Mrs. MacGregor is trying to make a game of Jimmy being sick.

I make my way to the kitchen, where the minister is pouring himself a cup of tea from a Brown Betty pot. There's a second cup for me. The minister raises an eyebrow in my direction.

"Yes, please."

I hug the teacup with my hands, hoping the warmth will thaw my toes and the fear around my heart. I need to brace myself for his questions. I must be on guard not to reveal anything that Aunt Jean wouldn't want me to say. I pull the sleeve of my blouse down so it covers the fingerprint bruises that are beginning to form around my wrist.

"What will you sing tonight?"

I'm flustered because it's not what I expect from a grown-up. I expect an inquisition about why Jimmy smells like drink. About who grabbed me.

The minister is asking me again what I'm going to sing. All that comes to mind is the song "Mairzy Doats."

I clap my hand over my mouth. Have I sung this bit of nonsense out loud? Have I? There's a smirk, a grin on the minister's face.

"I love that song," he says. "The men loved it. Sometimes in the mess, we'd sing it *just for the halibut.* It brings back memories, it does."

"You were in the war?"

"I served in the first war and was a chaplain in the second."

A chaplain in the war. Wow. No wonder Mr. MacGregor took in Jimmy and me. He'd seen far worse than one harum-scarum girl and her drunken friend landing on his doorstep on a dank evening at supper time.

I clear my throat. "Oh. I'll sing . . . whatever you'd like to hear."

"Do you have some sheet music with you?"

"Sheet music? Sheet music. Golly, I guess I forgot it at home."

Mr. MacGregor goes over to a drawer in the sideboard. He hands me several sheafs of music. "There might be something in here that strikes your fancy."

Some of the selections are yellowed with age. Some are newer, but all are popular songs that Grandpa used to sing from the war years. There's not a church song in the bunch. I flip through without speaking, getting lost in the selections.

"Your socks look wet. I'm going upstairs to find you another pair."

I've no idea how long he's been gone. I've been humming the first two bars of each song. I remember hearing these old songs on the radio.

"Find one you like?"

"Oh, yes. There are lots to choose from."

He gives me a pair of hand-knit socks, gray and chunky. They must have been warming on the radiator, because when my toes sneak down in, they wriggle with delight. Never mind they are men's socks and too big.

We can hear sloshing in the bathroom and Jimmy making motor-boat noises with his lips. Jimmy likes blowing bubbles.

"Jimmy seems happy now." The minister takes a big gulp of tea.

"Yes, he loves to play in the bath."

"My goodness, I'm hungry." The minister goes to the cookie jar and hands me two date oatmeal raisin cookies. "You won't tell on me, will you? Mrs. MacGregor won't like it if I spoil your dinner."

"I can keep a secret."

My response hangs in the air making an uncomfortable silence. I've learned that you don't have to fill uncomfortable silences. You don't have to rush to spill the beans. Eventually silences pass if you don't fall into the trap.

The minister speaks first. "Does your mother know where you are? Does Jimmy's mother?"

This is a trap question. If I say Aunt Jean wasn't at home when I got there, that will lead to Uncle Ted and the smell of liquor all over poor Jimmy. That will mean that the child welfare people might get called.

"Aunt Jean knows I wanted to try out for the choir," I say. It's a true statement. As far as it goes. I change the subject.

"Which of these two songs do you like better?" I sing the first two bars of "Don't Sit Under the Apple Tree" and switch to "I'll Never Smile Again."

In the silence after my singing, we hear the sounds of ripping fabric. The minister has a questioning look on his face, but I know what Mrs. MacGregor is doing. Jimmy is far too big for regular diapers and Mrs. MacGregor is making him new ones from sheets.

Did I say that right then and there, I said a prayer to God thanking him for leading us to Mrs. MacGregor? And for giving her about twenty kids of her own so she'd know what to do. I begin to relax.

I nibble around the edges of a cookie, savoring every morsel. Mr. MacGregor dunks his in his teacup.

"I think singing is important. I believe that mankind sang before it spoke," says Mr. MacGregor. "When I read the Creation Story, I sing it to myself." He takes another slurp. His cookie is getting mushy. "Yes, music, all music, every kind of music, has the power to speak to people everywhere, Carolyn. I discovered overseas that people aren't much different, dear, no matter where they happen to live. Egypt or Britain, or yes, even Germany. People want the same things. Family. Work. A roof over their heads . . ."

Aha! Clever man. He's enquiring again about my family. He wants to know where's the roof over Jimmy's and my heads, without coming out and asking.

I'm not biting.

When Jimmy runs out of the bathroom, his cheeks are apple red. His hair is damp and gleaming, but best of all, he smells like rosewater and talcum.

"My, you're a handsome lad," says Mr. MacGregor.

Jimmy smiles.

Mrs. MacGregor pours Jimmy a big glass of water.

"Slow down, Jimmy," I warn. "You don't want to spill on your new clothes." Jimmy's wearing a plaid flannel shirt with the sleeves rolled up and a pair of corduroy pants. He has fluffy pink slippers on his feet.

I can see that the dining room is set for dinner.

"It might be better if we eat in the kitchen," I warn. "We're not fancy folk."

Mrs. MacGregor and the minister lock eyes.

"I think you and your brother will be just fine in here," she says.

"He's not my brother." It sounds disloyal so I add, "He's my friend."

The minister continues lighting the candles on the table. He puts the record player on low, then turns the lights off. He helps Jimmy to his seat and me to mine.

Jimmy is mesmerized by the candles. He seems sleepy now, more old Jimmy than new Jimmy. He rests his head on the table and the minister tousles his hair.

The dinner is like a Sunday dinner. Roast potatoes and roast chicken. Squash, green beans, and yellow beans shiny with butter. There's raspberry pie and ice cream or apple crisp for dessert. Or both. Jimmy and I have both.

I remember my manners and scramble to clear the table.

"You don't need to help, dear," says Mrs. MacGregor. "You're our guest."

I take my dishes into the kitchen. Then I go back for Jimmy's and Mr. MacGregor's.

"Jimmy, do you have to use the toilet?" Normally, I don't take Jimmy to the bathroom, but I really don't want him to have an accident. These people are so nice.

I grab Jimmy's hand and begin to babble. "He needs an operation on his brain. Aunt Jean can't afford it. She tried to mortgage her house to pay for it, but her brother . . . well, there's already a mortgage on her house."

We all look at Jimmy. He smiles a goofy smile and twists his hands together.

"He used to be perfect," I say.

"I don't mind taking him to the toilet." Mrs. MacGregor reaches for Jimmy's hand. Mr. MacGregor clears his throat and pushes himself away from the table.

"May I please use the phone?" I'm worried about Aunt Jean. *What has Uncle Ted done with Aunt Jean?*

I dial the number. It rings and rings and rings. Ted finally answers. His speech is slurry.

I hang up without speaking. When I turn around, Mrs. MacGregor is watching me. She's been listening.

"Nobody is home," I lie.

Mrs. MacGregor hugs me to her and at first I'm stiff and unyielding. But Mrs. MacGregor is a force and I'm tired of struggling. I press my face into her apron that smells so sweetly of cinnamon. I concentrate on loving the feel of Mrs. MacGregor's plump, soft arms and pillowy bosom. I'm so tired that I think that in my mixed-up mind, I've substituted Mrs. MacGregor for Aunt Jean who is also very pillowy. *Where, oh where could Aunt Jean be?*

"Thank you for a lovely dinner, but I have to go now."

Mrs. MacGregor releases me.

"I'd better go."

I stand like I'm nailed to the linoleum floor.

"I'm going."

71

Mrs. MacGregor's voice turns from being motherly to all business.

"Of course you are, dear. Mr. MacGregor will take you to the audition. Jimmy can stay with me."

chapter

The minister helps me on with my coat. Jimmy doesn't make a whimper when I leave.

Mr. MacGregor whistles "Mairzy Doats" all the way to the church and I'm tempted to join in. I follow him up to the nave where a group of people are clustered around a piano. The minister speaks to the choirmaster who seems to be expecting me. I warm up with a couple of scales, then the piano player just starts playing the "Maple Leaf Forever."

I close my eyes and sing. There can be no thoughts of anything else now. Not *The* Bastard, not Uncle Ted, not anything. Until I'm done, I am completely unaware of how quiet the room has become. There's no coughing or throat clearing, just rapt attention.

I open my eyes. The adult choristers are beaming.

"Nicely done," the choirmaster says. "Carolyn, do you read music?"

"Oh, yes," I say. "I used to take piano lessons before my grandfather died, but now we can't afford them and since he died, I don't play much because it makes my mom sad. Besides, I'm always at Aunt Jean's." I'm gushing. I'm giving too much information. The minister and the choirmaster exchange looks before he asks, "Have you had any voice training, honey?"

"Only from my grandpa. He was a barbershopper. That's how my mom met my dad. He was a barbershopper too, but Grandpa didn't want my mom to marry him because, even though he sounded good, he was a real no-good."

I cover my mouth. What is *wrong* with me? I feel drunk and giddy, like Jimmy, but I haven't tasted a drop of whiskey. Mr. MacGregor is looking at me.

The choirmaster hands me a three-ring binder. I step into the choir, folded into the front row by lovely ladies with big chests and bigger smiles.

Let me say this about Christmas music. It is God-inspired. To think that a tiny baby with "no room for his head" grew up to save the world. It's a miracle, a great miracle that every year we celebrate His birthday.

Finally, we sing "Hark the Herald Angels Sing" and I sense that choir practice is ending. The piano player has moved to the organ. The building shakes with the power of that song and our voices. "God and sinners reconciled!" I know what reconcile means because I looked it up. It's like getting back together again, living in harmony, that kind of thing.

Uncle Ted is a sinner. I don't expect to ever reconcile with him. Maybe if he was struck by lightning and made stupid like our Jimmy, maybe then.

Uncle Ted is a rich man. He can afford an operation for Jimmy. He should reconcile his mistakes, instead of moving in and taking Aunt Jean's house right out from under her. He should make things right. Why doesn't God force him to do that? I wish I could ask Mr. MacGregor to explain, but I can't do that.

When all the people are putting on their coats and calling their good-byes, I approach the choirmaster. My heart is tapping allegro in my chest. *Can he hear it?* I take a big breath. "Do I have the job?"

"You certainly do. You'll make a lovely addition to our choir."

"I don't want to seem rude, but when do I get paid?"

He consults the note that Mr. MacGregor hands him. "Twice a month. But you must make every practice or forfeit a week's wages. I'll also dock you for bad behavior."

I make a face because there won't be any bad behavior from me. Not here. "Thank you. You can count on me."

Mr. MacGregor helps me on with my coat. I feel like Cinderella. I've forgotten our troubles for a few hours, but now they're back hitting me harder than ever. Aunt Jean. Jimmy. Ted.

"May I please use the phone when we get back?" I concentrate on using my best manners like Mom and Aunt Jean have taught me.

"Certainly."

I call Aunt Jean's. The line rings and rings and rings, then picks up. This time, there's only heavy breathing like someone has answered the phone by mistake or tucked the receiver under his chin.

I turn my back to the minister and whisper into the phone, "Where's Aunt Jean? Where is she? What have you done to her?"

Nothing but Ted breathing. I hang up the receiver.

"Sorry. No one's home, yet. My mom should be off at midnight. Sorry to be such a bother."

"Jimmy's sound asleep," says Mrs. MacGregor. "I made up a cot for you in the spare room."

"No, thank you," I say. "I'll just sit here and wait by the phone. I couldn't go to sleep."

"But tomorrow's a school day. You need your rest."

"My dear, why don't we let Carolyn lounge on the couch? I have work to do on my sermon."

"Yes, I can keep you company," I say. "I'd like to help."

Mrs. MacGregor hands me a pillow and a quilt.

The next thing I know, it's morning. When I open my eyes, my mom is crouching on the floor, peering at my face.

"Good morning, Sleeping Beauty," she says.

I struggle to piece it together. *Where am I? The rectory!*

"How did you get here?" I rub sleep from my eyes.

"Mr. MacGregor is a pretty good detective. He read the name tag Aunt Jean sewed in your coat. Then he called me after I got home."

I'm wide awake now. "Where's Aunt Jean?"

"In St. Joseph's Hospital."

"In the hospital? Why? Did she fall?"

"Sh, Carolyn. Calm down. Nothing like that. She was rushed in with internal bleeding. Woman's troubles. She needs an operation."

My voice rises hysterically. "Who's going to pay for that? Will they let her die if she can't pay?"

"Sh-hh-hh." Mom grabs my body and rocks me back and forth. "Calm yourself, you. Ted has taken care of everything. Ted will pay."

I'm relieved that Ted won't let Aunt Jean bleed to death. "When?"

My mom is confused. She thinks I mean when will Ted pay. "No. No, when will she have the operation. How long will she be in the hospital?"

"The operation is scheduled for this afternoon and she'll be in for eight to ten days."

"Ten days?" Ten days. I close my eyes and cover my ears, because I'm not sure I want to know the answer to my next question.

"And who'll look after Jimmy?" I whisper.

"It's all arranged. Jean says Ted has been wonderful. He's offered to stay with Jimmy. He can run his business from the kitchen table."

"I bet he can. Jimmy isn't going to like it."

What I mean to say is, *I* don't like it, and my mom knows me well enough to take my meaning.

"Carolyn, Carolyn, we don't have too many options here. We're not family."

Mr. MacGregor asks to speak to my mom while I wrestle Jimmy into his coat.

Staying with Ted is not an option! I scream this in my head. I don't say it out loud. After all, I'm in God's house. Or down the road from his house.

And what would be the point?

Ten Ted-days in a row! I think I'm going to be sick.

chapter

My mom has taken over Aunt Jean's kitchen and she's making a lot of noise washing up the dishes. She cleans like a crazy women when she's upset. Mom folds a tea towel and hangs it on the oven door and turns to me.

The rye bottle is not in the garbage can. I check. The lace table runner from the parlor has been rinsed out and is hanging on the back of a kitchen chair to dry. I take a sniff. It doesn't smell. Ted has covered his tracks.

"Ted will be home for dinner . . . regular time. He asked me to watch Jimmy until he gets back."

I make a face when I hear Ted's name. My mother brushes the hair out of her face. "I hope Jimmy will have a nap."

"He will if you will, Mom. He'll fall asleep in his bed if

you lie down beside him on the floor. It works every time. You can leave after he's fallen asleep and he won't care."

"You seem to be quite an expert. Maybe you should be helping out by doing some babysitting."

I want to say that I have all the babysitting I can handle with Jimmy, but that's not what she wants to hear. She doesn't want to know that she pays Jean to watch me and then I spend my time watching Jimmy. It's not supposed to be how it works.

Mom makes Jimmy and me French toast to use up the stale bread. It's our favorite. Jimmy likes it swimming in maple syrup but I prefer catsup. I mop my plate clean and there are only faint red streaks left on the plate.

Jimmy's a sticky mess with syrup in his hair and on his ear. I tense up thinking that Jimmy's going to get yelled at by my mom, but she only laughs.

"You've got to admit he's pretty cute," says Mom. I laugh with her. He's pretty cute and not so dumb really. He's been using the old typewriter to print words. His tongue goes around and around until he selects a letter before pushing it down firmly. Maybe I've been looking at Jimmy's letters too long, but they're beginning to make some sense to me. And his speaking is getting clearer.

For example, I'm pretty sure that *mk* means "milk."

"He wants milk!"

When my mom hands Jimmy a glass, he nods furiously and then drinks it down.

"Good work, Jimmy." I'm careful not to talk to him like a dog. Our Jimmy is a human being.

"It's time for school, Carolyn."

"I don't feel well."

"Sure you do. Look at the breakfast you just ate. Off you go."

"Are you going to stay home all day? You're not going to leave Jimmy for even one minute?"

"Why would I leave Jimmy?"

"I don't think Ted can handle Jimmy. I don't think he has the patience."

Mom is quiet. I can hear a housefly murdering itself inside the ceiling fixture.

"What am I supposed to do, Carolyn? I have a job. I can't lose my job. If I don't work, I don't get paid."

Now the fly sounds like he is murdering his best friend.

"Mom, I don't have to go to school. I've finished all the books. I have straight As. I can stay home and look after Jimmy."

"No you won't, little girl. No, you will not. Jimmy isn't your responsibility. Your responsibility is to get an education so that you never have to live like . . ."

"Us. . . ." I open and close my mouth like a goldfish around this little word.

There's no arguing with my mom. I know that a good job is everything. If Aunt Jean had a good job, she'd pay Uncle Ted back and throw him out on the street. We were just lucky that Grandpa took us in.

Money! Money! Money! It all comes back to money. Those who have it and those who don't. And oh, boy, you better not get sick or crack your head senseless because there might never be enough for that.

"Why don't you see how you feel by lunch time?" Mom's wheedling now. She thinks that if I make it until noon, I'll stay for the whole day.

She's plain wrong. I'll go to school, but I won't risk Ted coming back early. Ted will not get his clutches on Jimmy if I have one last breath in my chest.

Something will turn up. An idea will fall from the sky like a song. I'm sure of it.

chapter

Old Keezor catches me out in math. She's the first teacher in the history of time who's tripped me up in class, and I can see by the look on the horrid Luanne Price's face, it's a red-letter day for her. She's gloating. She sticks her hand up in Miss Keezor's face and answers the oh-so-simple question about isosceles triangles that I missed hearing because I was trying to force an idea.

Great ideas can't be forced. They have to be teased out.

That's how I find myself in the principal's office with a detention, which I'm to serve after school. That and shouting at the horrid Luanne Price to "Bug right off and mind your own business, you nosy pig." I *might* have called her "damn stupid" and I *could* have said "may you rot in hell" but I have no recollection.

There will be no "after school" for me today, so I listen politely to the lecture from the principal. Even if he puts me in stockades and handcuffs or threatens to throw me in debtor's prison, I will not be staying after school. I put on an attentive face, but I don't listen. The principal is a hypocrite. Even he seems to take delight in my fall from grace. That is what he calls it. He believes that although I'm doing very well academically, I'm working well below my potential because of my attitude.

He doesn't know that my attitude is about to get a lot worse.

"Now, I'm not going to call your mother and worry her as this is your first offence. But if it happens again, if you antagonize the children or your teachers in that way, I will have to call her in."

My mother won't come, you stupid horse-bun, I want to shout.

After I left for school this morning, I had to go back for *Jane Eyre*. I caught Mom crying in the bathroom. She told me she's putting aside half of her paycheck for Jimmy's operation. That's why she's working every shift she can get.

Did I say that I love my mom? Did I say that I wish she'd told me? Never mind.

Instead of answering the principal, I pretend I'm at a funeral and nod solemnly.

These days, I lead a double life, you see. They don't own my brain. No one owns my brain.

At lunch time, I pack my satchel.

"Where are you going?" Luanne Price asks.

"Home," I say. "I have a flu bug and a fever." I fake a sneeze in her direction and make sure that mucous flies out of my nose and lands on her sweater set.

"You are disgusting."

I smile sweetly.

My smile quells the flip-flopping in my stomach. I have no ideas. No ideas are falling from the sky as I walk home, just red maple leaves. I take a roundabout way home, passing by St. Olave's Church. Mrs. MacGregor is out raking leaves. I think I might march right by pretending that last evening didn't happen, but that would be impolite. It really would, after all her kindness.

"How is little Jimmy faring this morning?" she asks.

"Fair to middling. He misses his mom."

"And who will be caring for the lad, I'm wondering, now that she's in the hospital?"

"Uncle Ted." It pops out before I can stop it.

"I see."

Does she really see? Does anybody else see what I saw?

"This Uncle Ted would have to be an exceptional kind of man to look after the likes of Jimmy."

"He's exceptional," I say.

Mrs. MacGregor puts down her rake. She hands me the corner of an old bedsheet and together we haul the leaves to the ditch out front.

"We have an exceptional young man in our congregation who is waiting to go to divinity school next semester."

"You do?"

"And," says Mrs. MacGregor, "he's looking for a room to rent."

"He is?" I have stopped breathing now. Am I dreaming?

"And I think he and Jimmy would get along famously. It would be good experience for Andrew to interact with Jimmy on a daily basis, like a practicum."

"Really? Are you kidding me?"

"Carolyn, I'm not much of a teaser. I leave all the kidding in our household to Mr. MacGregor. Yes, I've already proposed the idea to Andrew and he likes it. It's fortuitous that you came along when you did. I haven't been able to reach your mother. The line is always busy."

"She takes the phone off the hook if she's sleeping. Could I ask a question, Mrs. MacGregor?"

"Yes, certainly."

"Is Andrew a big guy or a little guy?"

"A very big guy. He practices boxing."

"Oh-h-h," I breathe. "Thanks be to God." I'm unaware that I have said this out loud until I see the look on Mrs. MacGregor's face.

chapter

Mrs. MacGregor suggests that I wait while she fetches Andrew. I pick up the rake she's left leaning against the maple tree and begin rasp rasp rasping another pile. Would my mom like the whole idea? Would Uncle Ted throw Andrew out on his ear? I am playing a game of twenty questions when Andrew comes around the corner of the church with Mrs. MacGregor. His head, covered in black curlicues and absorbed in her every word, leans down toward Mrs. MacGregor's snow-white one. He moves like a dancer, lightly on the balls of his feet. I don't realize how big he is until he stands in front of me.

"This is Carolyn, lad, the girl I've been telling you about."

Andrew turns gray eyes on me and I have a flash of what it might be like to oppose him in the ring. He scares me, but then a great chuckle forms in his chest and rises up to make crinkles around his eyes.

"Nice to meet you, Carolyn. I hear you've got a job for me to do."

His smile knocks my breath clean away. I can't talk for the longest time until he taps my shoulder.

"Oh. A job. Yes. Well, it's more like babysitting, except Jimmy isn't a baby. And it's not up to me, really. You'll have to talk to ... well ... I guess Jimmy's Uncle. Uncle Ted."

"Anything I should know about this Uncle Ted?" Andrew has his hands in his front pockets and is rolling up on his toes. I glance at Mrs. MacGregor.

"No-o-o. Not really. Ted is just a ... well, Ted."

Mrs. MacGregor takes the rake out of my hands. Andrew shifts a canvas pack from one shoulder to the other like he's flicking a fly off his back. "Well, then. Why don't we just go and see the man about a job? Thanks, Mrs. MacGregor. I'll call you and tell you how I make out."

I'm so dithered, I forget to say good-bye to Mrs. MacGregor. "Well, uhmm, well, I don't think Ted's home yet. Ted's in plumbing supplies, you know, for homes and buildings and such. With all the new subdivisions being built, he's doing pretty well. I mean he drives a Thunderbird. Everybody calls him Uncle Ted." I'm babbling again.

"Wow. A Thunderbird. Neat-o. . . . So, what's your friend Jimmy like?"

I have to look away. I can feel my throat begin to close up because of his kindness. It has been a long time since anyone showed any interest in meeting our Jimmy. I can't speak. I keep my head turned away from Andrew and motion him to follow me. I feel like the pied piper leading the way to Aunt Jean's front door.

"This is it!" I shove it open.

Mom is in the kitchen peeling apples, and Jimmy is lying on the braided rug at her feet. He has his hand over his eyes and is watching the light from the ceiling fixture between the slits of his fingers.

"*MMM — NN-NNN*," he bellows.

"What's that, honey?" Mom tickles him with the toe of her slipper.

Andrew slips the bag off his shoulder and to the floor. He walks toward Jimmy and kneels down beside him.

"Hi, there, Jimmy. Are you looking at the moon?"

"*MMMMM-NN-NNNN!*" Jimmy is excited because Andrew has understood what he's been saying.

The paring knife falls from my mother's hand and clatters in the sink.

"Gracious! You scared me to death. And who might you be?"

"Sorry. I didn't mean to startle you, Mrs. Jamieson. Mrs. MacGregor sent me over to help watch Jimmy." Andrew shakes my mother's hand, but his eyes are for Jimmy. It's as if Jimmy is the only person that matters in the room, and it is left to me to whisper the details of the plan to my mom. Andrew puts his hands over his own eyes and peeks through his fingers at the ceiling fixture.

"Yes, Jimmy, I think that's the moon. A full moon. A real beaut."

My mom steps away and Andrew lies down on the kitchen floor. Jimmy scrunches closer to him and puts his head on Andrew's shoulder.

"My, goodness. I've never seen Jimmy take to anybody so quickly have you, Carolyn?"

I stand there like a guppy. Not since his accident or even before, has Jimmy taken to someone like this. For a second, I feel jealous of Andrew and how he has touched

Jimmy's heart so quickly. I'm prideful, as I said. And then Andrew motions me over and there we are, the three of us, lying on the kitchen floor, looking at the moon. Mooning over the moon, in Aunt Jean's kitchen.

I can tell my mom likes Andrew. We carry on madly as we lug his stuff up to my old room at Aunt Jean's place.

Jimmy tries to help as we change the sheets on my bed. We all land on the bed laughing, laughing, laughing so hard, I think my stomach will burst, or I'll wet my pants. We are laughing so hard, we don't hear Uncle Ted creep up the stairs. We don't notice him standing at the entrance of the bedroom. Not until Jimmy starts wailing and trying to hide himself under the bed.

"And what the hell is going on in here?"

I almost choke. It's what I said to Ted yesterday, almost exactly, minus "the hell" part.

Mom straightens her skirt.

"I said, what the hell is going on in here?"

"Gracious, Ted. I don't think there's any call for that kind of language. The kids were having so much fun we didn't hear you. Many hands make light work, you know. They are helping make up Andrew's bed. Oh. You don't know anything about this, do you now, Ted? Meet

Andrew Granger. He comes well recommended by Mr. MacGregor at St. Olave's. Isn't it wonderful? He's looking for a place to rent and has volunteered to look after Jimmy until Jean is on her feet." Mom smiles brightly. "Now Jimmy won't have to put you out at all. So, say hello. And will you stay to dinner? The minister and his wife are coming." I think Mom will never take a breath.

If looks could kill. Gas fumes seem to be coming from Ted's nose. Andrew holds out his hand first, and Ted swats it away.

"Jean doesn't need any Christian charity from you or the church. *I*, for one, know my family obligations."

My mother steps forward. "It's nothing like that, Ted. This opportunity just fell from heaven and I couldn't pass it up. It's all settled. Andrew is moving into Carolyn's room, here. And Carolyn and I will take over Jean's room. It's all been arranged. Jean is so happy to have the rent money from Andrew's lodging. . . ."

I can't believe what is coming from my mother's mouth. Did she just decide on the spot that we'd take over Aunt Jean's bedroom? Aunt Jean can't possibly know anything about Andrew.

"And I'm very glad to get room and board, sir. . . ."

"I bet you are, you interfering son-of-a –"

I know what is coming next. The purplish veins on Ted's nose look fit to burst, but he doesn't actually get to say a swear. Jimmy saves the day. He lets go a long and noisy fluff, which would have sent Jimmy and I into hysterics in the olden days before the accident. A black look of disgust passes over Ted's face to be replaced by a look that says as much as *you're welcome to the little so-and-so.* Ted turns on his heel and stomps down the stairs like he might snap each riser. The door slams so hard, the windows rattle.

"Do it again, Jimmy! Make a stinker!" Andrew tickles Jimmy's tummy. Another fluff, and we all fall on the newly made double bed. Even Mom.

It is all made funnier by the relief of it all.

Andrew can stay.

It turns out that the minister and Mrs. MacGregor aren't really coming for dinner at all. Mom says she made a little white lie to get Ted out of the house, and that she didn't really think Mr. MacGregor would mind. But as it turns out, it isn't quite a lie, after all, because Mr. MacGregor drops by for tea and cookies before he goes back home, just to see how we are all getting along. He even brings the cookies.

I could have hugged and kissed him, but I'm not the touching type. Partway through his visit, I notice that the knot of fear that has been growing in my stomach like a fur ball is gone.

For the moment, the clenching is gone. And now, as I look back, I wonder. If I hadn't let go of that clenching, would I have been better prepared for the next blow?

The jury's out. Maybe yes. Maybe no.

chapter

We settle into a nice little routine at Aunt Jean's. Between Andrew, Mom, and me, there are comings and goings all day and all night long. The only person who stays in place is Jimmy. For two weeks, there's no sign of Ted. Two Thursdays come and go and no Ted. I feel free enough to go to choir practice, confident that there will always be somebody to protect Jimmy. The adult choristers fuss over and pet me. Being the only kid, I'm an oddity. A specialty. I feel more at ease with them than any other people in the universe.

My solo performances in the choir somehow seem to help my public speaking. It's strange really. Everything is forward-looking – practicing carols for Christmas. Practicing my speech for November 11th. I don't really remember much about Thanksgiving, except at dinner Ted had too much to drink and made remarks that Mom said were very inappropriate. Something about the meal being the Last Supper. After that, Ted stopped coming over every Thursday.

You might think that I'm glad not to see his ugly face. I am, but now I have to worry every day of the week about when he might pop up. At least before, I could relax until Ted-day. My mom says I'm like a border collie, always nipping at her heels and Andrew's heels to make sure that someone is going to be at home for Jimmy. Always.

On two Saturdays, Jimmy and I walk over to St. Joseph's Hospital. My mom has arranged with Aunt Jean that she'll sit in the lounge at one o'clock and Jimmy and I will be outside on the lawn. I count up five storeys and along to the end window. I point out Aunt Jean to Jimmy and he is so excited. We wave and wave and do goofy stuff on the lawn, like somersaults and play sword fighting. We try to put on a show for Aunt Jean to amuse her. She looks like an old lady up there sitting in a rocking chair watching us but, of course, she's in a wheelchair. My mom says that Aunt Jean is recovering well from her operation, but she'll have to rest when she comes home.

Her homecoming day is crazy with housecleaning. Jimmy picks up on the excitement, even though we don't tell him what is going to happen. Andrew's in charge of moving the furniture and I dust and vacuum. Jimmy tears around the place like a terrier, getting into trouble and in the way.

My mom makes homemade bread and Scotch broth for nourishment. There's a batch of oatmeal raisin cookies and some old-fashioned current scones. And butter tarts.

Everything looks quite sparkly for Aunt Jean's arrival. Jimmy and I cut some snapdragons that are growing beside the house and have managed to escape the frost. We arrange them in a pint milk bottle and place them on the kitchen table. It all looks very homey.

Ted picks up Aunt Jean in his car and brings her home. He and Andrew make a seat with their hands and lift Aunt Jean up the stairs and onto the verandah. Once there, she shoos them away.

"I can enter my *own* house under my *own* steam, thank you very much." She wavers at the threshold of the front hall, gripping the doorjamb for support.

Jimmy is sitting on the stairs playing jacks.

"*Mm-ahn!*" he bellows. I grab his braces and hold on, fearful that he will run at Aunt Jean and knock her down. She's so skinny and pale, her legs like Popsicle sticks peeking out from a black wool skirt. But her face softens when she sees Jimmy and tears stream down her face. Her lips are moving, but I can't hear the words because of Jimmy's bawling.

"Sit down Jimmy!" I haul him down on the last stair and half sit on him to keep him in place. "Jimmy, let Aunt Jean get into the kitchen! If you knock her over, you'll land her right back into the hospital and we can't afford that, can we?" I can hear a chair scraping on the linoleum in the kitchen as Aunt Jean settles.

Andrew comes back to the vestibule for Jimmy. He lifts him in the air, clamping Jimmy's flailing arms to his side. Then he swoops Jimmy's face down close to Aunt Jean's head. She grabs that poor boy's neck and smothers him with kisses. Wet, teary kisses.

Jimmy bellows.

"Mommy has a hurt," says Andrew. "Gentle. Gentle." Andrew lets go of one of Jimmy's hands and guides it to Aunt Jean's shoulder. Jimmy paws at her shoulder making sure she's real. My mom helps Jean off with her hat and coat. Her galoshes.

"Will you stay for dinner, Ted?" my mother asks. She says it coldly, just to be polite.

"Much as I'd love to, I have things to do."

I can see Aunt Jean muscling herself together and sitting up straight. "Thank you, Ted, for bringing me home. It's so much better to be in my own house. I've been looking forward to my own bed." Aunt Jean stresses the word *own*. It's her new favorite word.

That night, it seems strange to be back in *my* own bed on *my* own side of the shared wall. Just me and my very *own* mom. In the morning, it's luxurious to stretch like a cat, touching right to the bottom of the bed with my toes and wiggling them under the blankets. It's all so new that it takes me a while to realize that something has changed in the night. The light's too bright and too soft in my room.

Snow! The first snowfall! I rip open the curtains. The street is silent and lumpy and clean and so white like someone has rolled out a cotton batting carpet. My heart leaps high with excitement. There are things to be thankful for. I mean, Aunt Jean's home. Andrew's like Jimmy's new big brother looking out for him, only better, because he pays rent. I close my eyes tight. *Thank you, God.*

When I open my eyes, I see what I didn't see before.

Boy, oh boy. Ted meant it last night when he said he had things to do.

There's an orange and white sign right in the middle of Aunt Jean's lawn. Some time after we'd gone to bed, Ted pounded a FOR SALE sign into Aunt Jean's frosty grass!

I feel a spasm in my stomach so deep and so cold, it travels all the way to my toes.

Our Jimmy will be moving away from me.

It's true. I have to believe it. Ted is selling Aunt Jean's house right out from under her! How can he do this? To his own sister? And her so sick and just home from the hospital!

Bastard.

Ted's a bastard. And I don't care anymore who knows it.

chapter

When Mom sees the sign, she puts her coat on over her flannelette pajamas. She stuffs bare feet into boots and slams our front door so hard that both houses shake. I watch from the front window as she tries tugging the sign out of the ground. Then she tries to knock it over with one good kick. Finally she grabs the garden rake and swings it like a baseball bat, splintering bits of wood across the lawn. She stuffs the sign and what's left of the stake into our garbage can. Then the two of us troop over to Aunt Jean's for coffee and breakfast.

Mom goes into the kitchen to put on the kettle. She's making a big, big racket in there.

I discover Aunt Jean dressed and dozing in a chair in the parlor. The curtains are drawn and there's only a faint glow of orange coals in the fireplace to warm the room. Poor Aunt Jean. She looks wizened and old, her mouth open, her glasses, which usually hide some of the puffiness under her eyes, rest on an end table. Gently, I tuck a quilt around her.

She stirs, but doesn't open her eyes. "Is . . . that . . . you . . . dear?" Every word has a sigh and a pause in it as if there's just too much — too, too much effort required to form the word and push it out of her mouth.

"Yes, Aunt Jean. Guess what? It snowed last night. It's a winter wonderland outside."

"I know dear. I . . . saw . . . it. . . ."

We both know we are not talking about the snow but the FOR SALE sign. A single tear leaks from her eye, catches in a wrinkle furrow, slips off her chin and onto her bosom.

"I wonder if he'll let us stay until Christmas."

"Where will you go?" I whisper. I can't imagine what the answer to this question will be.

Nor can Aunt Jean. "Help me up, dear."

I brace her under the elbow and lever her to a standing position. I think that my shoulder will crumple with the weight of her body leaning on mine.

Aunt Jean is distracted at breakfast. She manages one

bite of toast and a sip of tea that I lift to her lips. I look at my mother for help. She shrugs her shoulders as if to say "What can I do? What can anybody do?"

Aunt Jean smacks the table top with her two palms. "I want to go to church."

I know she's in no condition to go to St. James. I beg her to come with me to St. Olave's instead. "It's not far. You can hear me singing. I'm in the choir and I have to get going pretty soon."

"Jean, be realistic," Mom says. "You aren't well enough to travel downtown on the streetcar. Let me call Ted and he can drive you."

"Over my dead body!" There are no pauses in Aunt Jean's words now. They come out in a rush.

Aunt Jean agrees to a compromise. She'll rest all day and she and I will take a cab to the streetcar loop in time to catch evensong at St. James. That way, she can save her energy and her pennies. While we're gone, Mom will stay home with Jimmy and they can catch a nap.

At three o'clock, Aunt Jean's dressed and waiting for me. She's applied some powder and lipstick to her face, which only makes the paleness of her skin more pronounced. She's dressed in black from top to bottom and smells faintly of mothballs. The netting from her old hat is askew. There's nothing fashionable about what Aunt Jean is wearing today. She's no competition for the Rosedale ladies.

The taxi man is kind. He speaks with an Italian accent, but he turns the meter off and waits quietly until the King car arrives so Aunt Jean won't get chilled. He helps her up the stairs. She gives him a coin from her purse and I can tell he's surprised. He doesn't expect a tip from a sick lady who is clearly so poor.

Outside the cathedral, the bells are rocking, rocking so exuberantly that I imagine them whipping horizontally back and forth, calling Aunt Jean and me to pray.

Come in. Come on.
Come in. Come on.

Surely, the bells can be heard all the way to Swansea.

People stream into the church and I'm surprised at the number of parishioners. The sunlight flickers weakly through the stained glass. The church is drafty. The candles wavery and smoky. When the bells finally stop and the organ takes over with a funereal dirge, I want to weep, but as I said, I'm not the weeping kind. Instead, I roll, I twist my lace gloves in my hands until they resemble one of Jimmy's bedsheets, "warshed" clean of urine and squeezed dry of soap and water, ready for the clothes line.

"Let us pray."

It's a luxury to sit in my seat beside Aunt Jean listening to the Men and Boys Choir. Evensong is all about music and I don't have to be interrupted once to check up on Jimmy. I'm glad we've left Jimmy home. I feel a prickle of guilt thinking that, and then it's gone with one phrase of celestial notes.

The boys – just the boys, mind – chant all on one note. I find myself putting words to the tones. Not the Latin words of the magnificat, but ordinary words with weight and melody. "Lin – ol – e-um-mm-mmm-mmmn. Win – der – me – re-re-re-re. Thun – der – bir-d-d-d-d-d." These three- and four-syllable words don't sound like nonsense when chanted. They make about as much sense as the words in Latin coming from the boys' mouths. Do they know what they're singing? Some of them are so young, they can't know how to read music. How do they sing at all?

"Di-ap-per-s-s-s. Un-der-wear-r-r-r. Tor-on-to-o-o-o-o." Words with natural interval changes. Words to play with. Words for rhythm, for nonsense. "El-bow. El-bow to that!" *El-bow* makes as much sense as *A-men*, musically speaking. What does *Amen* mean? Where does it come from? Grandpa would know. That's exactly the kind of thing he would have been able to tell me, but he's dead now. The boys might as well be singing "H-um-ber," a soft-sounding name for the river that winds its way to Lake Ontario.

Lost in this kind of thinking, I'm startled when the General opens our box and sits down with us. I didn't know he came to the evening service, too. He nods at Aunt Jean and gives me a wink. He's rubbing his hands together with excitement. He's *so* glad I've come. He whispers in my ear that a good old friend of his from out west is preaching tonight. That's why the church is so full, he tells me. There'll be history in the making tonight, according to the General.

The General does the "reading" from the Bible. While eyes flash from face to face. He's memorized his contribution. After he's finished, there's much clucking and coughing and rustling of clothes in anticipation of the guest speaker delivering the sermon. I check my sheet.

The Right Honourable, the Right Reverend Tommy C. Douglas, Premier of Saskatchewan.

I've never heard of him, but Aunt Jean has. There's a spot of color in her cheeks and she's gripping her purse so tightly, you'd think someone was trying to snatch it from her.

Mr. Douglas grips the side of the lectern and jumps right into his speech about Christianity and war, because as he says, November the 11th is just around the corner. We'd better not forget.

"In the Western world we are spending billions of dollars on implements of destruction. I am not a pacifist and I do not think that in a troubled world like ours it is advisable to be defenseless. The fact remains, however, that bombs and guns are not the final answer. I believe that in the long run love is stronger than hate, kindness better than cruelty, and a helping hand more powerful than the clenched fist."

Mr. Douglas's fist is raised in the air and he thumps it hard on the podium. There is a long silence before he continues.

"I have often wondered what would happen if we were prepared to take 25 percent of what we were spending on armaments and devote it to the task of feeding and clothing the hungry people of the world. If we were prepared to take some of the great food surplus we have or some of our great supplies of farm machinery and electrical generating equipment, and make them available to the people of the underdeveloped countries, I venture the faith that an action of that sort would do more to establish peace and good will in the world than all the bombs and guns we will ever produce."

There's no sound in the church now, and Mr. Douglas takes off his glasses and points at us with them. I feel like he's speaking to me alone at the kitchen table over a cup of tea and oatmeal cookies.

"We must constantly ask ourselves why nations go to war. What is it that drives men to attack their neighbors? The whole story of history reveals the fact that when people get hungry they become desperate and they will follow any leader that offers them bread –

even if it is their neighbor's bread. How long do we think we can maintain peace in a world in which the Food and Agriculture Organization of the United Nations estimates that fifteen hundred million people go to bed hungry every night?"

People are rustling now. Could there be fifteen hundred million hungry people in the world? I mean *really* hungry, not just like me and my mom who have beans and eggs for dinner sometimes when we're waiting for the next paycheck?

"One of the greatest presidents of the United States once said that no nation can long survive half slave and half free. I am suggesting tonight that the world cannot long survive half full and half hungry. Peace is only possible where men have learned the principles of co-operative living, and where we are prepared to share with those less fortunate than ourselves . . ."

I'm like a sleepwalker leaving the cathedral. I don't protest when the General offers to drive us all the way home. I listen to the General tell Aunt Jean how disappointed he is that Tommy Douglas didn't talk about Medicare – free health care for all.

He pats Aunt Jean's hand. "Too political a topic for him at church, I guess, with all those Rosedale Tories sitting in the pews. I'll take you to a rally, Jean. Oh, how he can get a crowd going."

I don't listen to Aunt Jean and the General discussing her troubles. I don't even flinch when I see a new FOR SALE sign pounded into Aunt Jean's front lawn.

Doctors for free? My head spins with the oratory, the persuasiveness, and the good sense of this Premier of Saskatchewan, this former Baptist minister.

I'm half full and half hungry, for more of his words. For more of his ideas.

chapter

If it wasn't for the cardboard boxes packed and shoved under the bed and the occasional young couple touring the house, I'd forget that Aunt Jean and Jimmy have to move. Where they will go has been decided. Uncle Ted has an investment property in Mimico. They'll live above a hardware shop. And as much as it galls Aunt Jean to take charity from the likes of Ted, the price is right. Free. She'll have none of moving in with us. After we make the bread for the week, Mom and I are going to visit the apartment to see what needs to be done. After we do our chores.

My mother bakes the most heavenly bread. I help her assemble all the ingredients. The flour. The butter. The cake of yeast. The sugar. The salt. A clean tea towel. A big bowl for mixing. And then I stay out of her way. My favorite part is the kneading. I pretend to read a book, but mostly I sneak peeks at my mother. There's a sheen of perspiration on her upper lip. Her arms quiver like junket. I know not to disturb her until the minute-minder dings to say that ten minutes is up. Mom is a stickler for kneading bread ten minutes precisely. She's experimented and this seems to work best.

The bread is elastic but firm when she's done. Four loaves. Two for Jimmy and two for us. Side by side, they look like the buttocks of twin babies, plump and rounded. Mom always gives them a little love pat and they jiggle like a baby's bum too.

"That's that!" she says.

It's my job to cover them with an ironed tea towel and set them by the radiator. I use exactly the same place my grandmother did, in the front vestibule before you go up the stairs.

My mom is much more relaxed after she's kneaded bread. The process calms her. I put the kettle on the stove. While I wait for the whistle, I take a fancy plate from Grandma's dining-room hutch and two English bone china cups and set them on the oil cloth of the kitchen table. There are day-old Chelsea buns in the bun warmer and the smell of sugar and cinnamon is sending signals to my stomach.

The time after my mother kneads bread is the only time in the week that I can talk to her and be sure that she'll answer my questions. Otherwise, there are too many things to do with shift work and housecleaning and laundry and trying to catch up on some sleep. I have big questions to ask her because I need to understand about Ted.

I warm the teapot with boiling water and swish it around to make sure it's good and hot. I fill the silver tea ball with tea leaves and hook the chain over the rim of the pot. The kettle is shrieking on the stove but I dare not move it off the element until everything is ready. The water must be roiling boiling to make the best tea.

I put raspberry jam Thumbelina cookies on the plate. Jimmy and I made them when we were little, and we were allowed to push our thumbs into every cookie before the jam was spooned in. I called them our little Thumbelinas and the name stuck.

My mom and I sit across from each other. She pours milk into the cups, way more for me, and then from a height, pours the tea. She takes three sips and sets down her teacup in the saucer.

I pass her the plate of cookies.

"Now, tell me about your whole life, lovey."

Normally, we talk about school. Or what I'm reading. She doesn't get much time to read anymore so I tell her stories. She likes mysteries. But today, as I said, I have a different plan. Today, we are going to talk about Ted.

"What was Ted like when he was a kid?"

My mom peers at me over the rim of the cup. She's considering why I'm asking these questions. Why now?

"He was all right. He was considerably older than I. Bertie and I were more of an age, although even he was four years older. We tobogganed in the park and skated, of course, for hours on end. Ted was very protective of Bertie. He really took it to heart that he was the uncle. Ted was seven when Bertie was born. That's how come everyone calls him *Uncle* Ted. The name stuck, I guess because he was an uncle at such an early age."

"A seven-year-old uncle seems silly."

"Yes, well it happens. Ted and Bertie might have been brothers, really. Jean and her husband, Jake, worked long hours getting the hardware business up and running, so Jean's mother watched them. Those were hard years, making enough money to buy the house next door. And we know how that turned out."

"So, Ted used to be a nice enough guy?"

My mom makes a face like the tea is scalding her mouth. "He was okay. He was good with his hands. Always building and fixing stuff. It doesn't surprise me that he's done well in the building trade."

"So what happened? How come he's such a crank now?"

"I'm not absolutely sure. I know that Ted had a falling out with Bertie when Bertie enlisted in the service. Ted had been turned down flat because of his feet. Folks say that it galled Ted that his nephew went off to war and not him."

"It was like they changed places."

"I guess. Really, it's a closed book. Jean won't talk about it."

I pull apart a Chelsea bun and nibble around the edges like a mouse. "What do you think really happened?"

"I don't know, Carolyn. You ask too many questions. All I know is, there's more to the story." My mother stands and begins clearing up the tea things leaving me to ponder how anybody could be mad that they didn't get to go to war, especially when the person who did go to war got shot down dead. How could you stay angry about that all these years later? As I said before, boys can be so dumb. They can be dumb about Thunderbird convertible cars. And they can be dumb about war.

We take a bus and a streetcar and another bus to get to Mimico and Aunt Jean's new apartment. It's like we are in another city altogether.

We have to walk up a narrow flight of stairs to get to the apartment. The lock on the door looks flimsy, but it opens easily enough when Mom turns the key. The walls are dark green and sunlight only comes in through the front and back windows of a very long and narrow space. There's one toilet, mean and rusted, and a tiny back kitchen with an ancient stove and peeling linoleum. The kitchen is filthy and stinks of cabbage and onion. My mom runs her fingers along the window ledge, peeling and black with mold.

"A coat of paint or three will help get this place ship shape." I can tell that Mom is attempting to be brisk and efficient and positive thinking.

I stand by the window that overlooks a gravel parking lot. As far as the eye can see, there are laneways and rusting tin roofs. No grass. NO safe place to play.

"Jimmy won't like this," I say.

"Neither will Aunt Jean. There are no flowers or trees."

"I hate Ted." I say it matter-of-factly as an honest expression of how I feel. Mom doesn't reproach me. "Besides, there's a big problem."

"What?" Mom asks.

"There's no laundry room."

My mom lets out a long breath. Both of us are trying to visualize Aunt Jean wrestling with Jimmy's daily sheets and diapers, stowing them in the rusty old bathtub and then lugging them to the launderette way down the street.

"It's not fair," I say.

"Life is not fair, Carolyn, love. I'm sorry that there are some things I just can't change."

I don't accept that. I will not accept that. I'd rather die than accept that. Every day I struggle with how *I* can make things better for Aunt Jean and Jimmy. How can I, a kid, make something good happen for them? I know that my measly choir money, which I save in my piggy bank, will never do it. But it's a start. As Aunt Jean says, if you look after the pennies, the pounds will take care of themselves. One day I will, I WILL have enough to pay a doctor to help Jimmy. If you don't believe me, just watch.

And when I'm done worrying about Aunt Jean and Jimmy, I worry about me. What's going to happen to me when Mom goes to work? Who's going to take care of me? Aunt Jean will be in another school district entirely. I can't take streetcars there every day after school and then back in the morning. It's not sensible. Not sensible at all.

I feel guilty for thinking about me in the face of their troubles.

Mom picks up some newspaper and garbage littering the postage-patch of weeds outside the apartment door. She introduces herself to the hardware store owner but I stay outside on the sidewalk with my back to the building.

It's all I can do to sweet-talk myself into being positive. This is just a lay-by for Jimmy and Aunt Jean. And me, of course. We'll get through.

chapter

One day in early November the principal calls me to the office.

What now? I think. I scan my behavior for something that might have attracted his attention. The missed detention blew over quite nicely with a forged note from my mom about possible symptoms of influenza. I'd hoped they'd have a big meeting to decide whether to shut down the school, but no. No such luck.

Apparently, now I'm too quiet. Too reserved. Not my usual self and all the teachers have reported this to him. Is there something wrong at home he should know about?

Yes there is something wrong at home. Everything is wrong at home, I scream in my head, but I'm not about to tell anything to this hypocritical man who only last week reveled in my first offence. There's nothing he needs to know.

"No, Sir."

He switches the subject and tells me how much he's looking forward to my speech. He's heard from my teacher that it's very dramatic and patriotic. It will be a lovely addition to the Remembrance Day celebration, he's sure.

I thank him and turn to leave the office.

"There's one more thing, Carolyn. I've been asked by someone at the City to send a speaker to the cenotaph. I wondered how you might feel about that?"

"Gosh."

My mind is racing. Aunt Jean will be there. If I do my speech at the cenotaph, I'll be able to be with Aunt Jean. But it will mean that I'll have to give my talk twice in less than two hours.

"I don't mind."

"That's settled then. I'm sure you'll be a fine ambassador for the school,"

No. No, Sir I will not. These days, I don't care two figs about the school or about you. I'm looking after myself, like I always have, but more so since Jimmy fell. I'll be a fine ambassador for myself and my mom and Aunt Jean and Jimmy, but that's it.

I'm sure you're wondering about my speech. I've heard it said the thing that people fear more than death is public speaking. I suppose it's true, but I don't see how. I don't think much about public speaking, myself. Mom says that people are shocked that a little kid like me can do public speaking like a pro. What she doesn't say, but I know she thinks, is that I'm a chip off the old bastard. I think my father must have been an actor as well as a singer. He sure tricked my mom.

Never mind. We'll never know.

I practice my speech after dinner every night in front of the mirror. I concentrate on timing and gesturing and pausing in the right places. Nobody has taught me to do this. It just happens.

November moves along, dark, drizzly, and November-ish. On the evening of November 10th, I'm at Aunt Jean's. Andrew has taken Jimmy for a walk up to the church. I'm about ready to have a bubble bath, even though it isn't Sunday. Part of public speaking is looking confident, and I want to be as confident and sweet-smelling as I can be. After all, I have to deliver my speech twice – once at nine o'clock at the school, and then at eleven o'clock at the cenotaph. The principal offered to drive me down, but I said, "No thank you." The General's picking up Aunt Jean and I'll go with them.

The doorbell rings at 8:30 p.m.

"Carolyn, get the door, please!" Aunt Jean hollers. "I'm on the phone."

"I'm drawing a bath!"

"I don't care if you're drawing the Mona Lisa!"

I thunder down the stairs, turn on the porch light, and flip the bolt on the door.

Luanne Price is standing on the porch flanked by three adults. "What are you doing here?" I ask.

A man in a suit and tie presents his real-estate card.

"You don't live here," says Luanne.

"No. For once, Luanne, you're right. I live next door. What are you doing here?"

My mind is racing. Are Luanne Price's parents considering buying Aunt Jean's house?

"My mother and father want me to see if I like this house before they put in an offer."

The agent barges right in. They don't take off their shoes. I trail behind them.

"Carolyn, do you have water running?" Aunt Jean calls.

I race ahead up the stairs. Phew, I'm lucky. The bubbles are mounding over the top of the tub, but not the water. I reach in and pull the plug, draining some of the excess away.

Luanne and her family are in Jimmy's room now.

"Pee-yew!" Luanne says, holding her nose. "I can't sleep in here."

The real estate man pipes up. "This room can be professionally steam cleaned and painted."

"You mean fumigated," says Luanne's father.

Now, the upstairs hallway in Aunt Jean's house is very narrow with really only room for two people at a time. So it's possible that I could have accidentally brushed past Luanne Price, knocking her off balance. Sadly Luanne has no balance at all, or maybe my brushing was more like a rugby hit, but no matter. Luanne stumbles and skins her knee on the hardwood floor.

"Sorry. Sorry." I help her up.

"Don't touch me." She makes a sign like she's warding off evil spirits. She makes the same sign toward Jimmy's room.

I follow them downstairs. The real-estate man shakes my hand or tries to. Luanne is being spiteful. She does what comes next to get at me. She must know that she's the last person on earth I would want to share my semi-detached house with.

"I like it. Let's buy it."

As they are walking out the door, the salesman says, "The vendor needs to sell. It's a forced sale. The house doesn't show well. I'm sure you'll get a rock-bottom price." He's talking like I'm not even there.

"Bug off, Luanne Price!" She hears me. I slam the door on their backs. And turn off the porch light.

I hope they fall down the stairs and break their necks.

chapter

It's November the 11th. Remembrance Day. I'm in my own bed in my own house trying not to remember the horror of last night. The horrid Luanne Price living right next door!

I roll over and look at the floor. Last night before I went to bed, I laid a sheet on the carpet and assembled my outfit for today. My mom is not nearly the cleaner that Aunt Jean is. Or was, before she got so sick. Things are slipping next door.

Never mind.

When you do public speaking, it's very important how you look. I don't have a uniform to wear, but I've chosen something to make me look as military as possible. A white, long-sleeve shirt like a boy-shirt. My navy skirt.

A navy cardigan with brass buttons. Navy kneesocks and black Oxfords – shiny black.

The cardigan has a little breast pocket and I've folded a very elegant white handkerchief in there. Now, normally, I'd wear a regular poppy on Remembrance Day, but those are too small to be seen from the back of the room. I've made my own from scrap felt in Aunt Jean's sewing box. My poppy is as big as my fist which is as big as my heart. I pin it on the pocket of my cardigan.

The final piece of my costume – and it is a costume – is a soft red cap with a peaked brim. It's warm and blood-red. Perfect for a speech about dead men and war and why I'm proud to be Canadian.

I hear movement next door. Aunt Jean will also wear a costume today. Her costume is black. That is what the Silver Cross Mother wears when she represents all the mothers in the province whose children have died in war.

I walk to school alone so that I can say my speech in my head. I consider the speech at the school to be a kind of warm-up for the cenotaph. In the hallway at school, the kids ask me if I'm nervous, which is enough to make anybody nervous but, no. I'm not nervous. I'm excited. I love to perform. And this is a winning speech. My hope is that they'll all be crying their eyes out at the end.

I won't bore you with the text of my speech – it's changed fifty times since I first wrote it because I used to blubber right through it for real. But I'm happy to tell you that they like it. When I stop speaking, when I reach for that lace handkerchief and dab at my eyes as if I'm crying, there is absolute silence. And then sniffling and then sobbing from the teachers that transfers like electricity to the girls. And then some of the boys are shuffling their feet and looking down.

It's all I can do not to laugh with relief, but a speech about why you are proud to be Canadian on Remembrance Day is a somber thing. It's not a laughing matter. Besides, there are things I can improve upon. When I talk about Flanders Fields and the crosses and the bodies of our boys from the farms lying in their graves side by side like bales of hay, my voice should waver like the blowing wind. I want them to picture those white crosses, row on row and the blood-red poppies.

Never mind.

I can do better.

chapter

I'm beginning to suspect that the General is behind the selection of Aunt Jean as the Silver Cross Mother.

I sit in the backseat of the General's Ford, eyes closed as the General and Aunt Jean talk quietly up front. Andrew sits in the middle with Jimmy up against the window so he can look out. I don't have to babysit Jimmy today and I block out his bellowing.

As we rush downtown in the General's car, my mind rushes over all the things that have happened to Jimmy since Uncle Ted bucked him out of the car. So many changes since that split instant when Jimmy hurt his head.

"Are you all right, Jean? You're awfully pale." There's concern in the General's voice.

"Just a little weak. I'll be all right. Too many memories, I guess."

"Maybe we should have gotten you a wheelchair."

"Over my dead body!"

It's her latest and most favorite saying particularly when Ted's name comes up. It never ceases to grab me by the heart and stop my breath. What would happen to Jimmy if Aunt Jean died? I shake this thought from my head.

I know I don't need to tell you this. It always drizzles on November the 11th. It's like the atmosphere is holding back a dam of tears and will just let them leak out a few at a time. Softly like the clouds are trying to gulp them back and not let them show.

The General has a VIP pass. He's driving the VIP person of the day and we park in a special spot. An airman in uniform opens our door. The General salutes. The General helps Aunt Jean out of the car and tucks her arm in his. For a moment I wonder if the General could be sweet on Aunt Jean, but no, he's probably just being polite.

Jimmy and Andrew trail behind, being introduced through a receiving line of dignitaries. I ask a veteran where the choir is assembling. Before I go, I give Jimmy's hand a squeeze. "Be good, Jimmy. Clap when I've done my speech. When it's over, mind, not in the middle." He bellows something I take to mean good luck. I run and find a seat.

There's a sea of people, most wearing dark colors so there's no trouble finding the choir. They're dressed in crimson robes. "Hi, Carolyn. Hi, Carolyn." Many of the choir members sing at St. Olave's too. It's comforting to see them. They're too professional to ask if I'm nervous. I'm not nervous. I'm a racehorse at the gate.

I don't know, frankly, what makes me stand in front of all those people and say the things I do. I don't plan it, that's for sure. I am following the set speech and the next thing I know, well . . . I don't know precisely what tips the balance for me. Maybe it's Aunt Jean leaning heavily on the General's arm, looking so pale and tired like a wrung-out dishrag. Or maybe it is Jimmy tugging at his pants, rearranging his diapers and Andrew trying desperately to distract him. Possibly it's the proud and expectant faces of my friends in the choir, standing off to the side. Supporting me.

I picture Bertie's plane exploding into bits and hitting the water of the English Channel.

I picture the horrid Luanne Price stretched out along the shared wall of our semi-detached house, inches from my body. Where Jimmy has always slept.

I see Uncle Ted who, as I stand at the podium organizing my notes, I catch out of the corner of my eye, slinking behind the crowd, positioning himself so he can see Aunt Jean when she goes up to place the wreath. Without her knowing he is there.

You have no right to be here. You have no right. I swallow these words and they stick in my throat.

I don't understand why Ted continues to be so horrid to Jimmy. I mean, if it was me that hurt someone, I'd be trying to make it up somehow. Ted's a coward. He reminds me of a dog who has been kicked around, the kind that crawls toward you on its knees and won't come close for fear you might yell at him to be off. A mangy mutt, slinking low with tail down. I watch Ted circle the circle of people before me. They are holding their black umbrellas so that they touch one another to form a black honey-combed canopy. Everyone is cold and wet and dripping.

During the minute of silence, everyone's head is bowed. Except Ted's. He is on the move. He is craning to look over the umbrellas, wedging himself here and there, trying to get a better view of . . . what? Aunt Jean? The placement of the wreath? *What?*

I observe my minute of silence from behind the microphone. From this height, I can look down and be respectful and still see Ted scuttling. He's wearing his driving cap. A spot of white wending its way ever closer, as he pushes through the corkscrew maze. He is standing a car length behind Aunt Jean now. But he is watching me. Me.

Ted only has eyes for me. He is as close to me now as I ever want him to be.

Oh, no! It's my turn to speak. The sea of people in black and navy and brown swim in front of my eyes and then settle down. I clasp my hands together as if I'm about to sing. I open up my mind and my heart to speak. But these are not the words on the paper. I can't see the words on the paper, I recite from memory and then, like I said, something changes.

These are the words of God coming out of my mouth. Or Tommy Douglas. Or both. You see, I'm not exactly sure what I do say. I'm not aware that I've memorized part of Tommy Douglas's sermon. Now Tommy Douglas's voice is pounding out of my body. I pound the podium and point at the people assembled.

I talk about my Aunt Jean, the Silver Cross Mother and how her son Bertie would have been her means of support if he'd lived. But he was cut down over the English Channel and lost for good. Forever. Leaving behind an old and sick widow with a child who needed an operation. And no money to pay for it.

The honor and the dignity of being the Silver Cross Mother is nice and all that but it does not change the fact that when Aunt Jean goes home tonight, there is no money to save her from being thrown on the street with her suitcases.

"In post-war times, this country is so busy trying to forget. Trying to forget by purchasing TVs and radios and cars. Thunderbird convertible cars. What's a Thunderbird convertible car compared to the life of a child, a normal healthy child who, through no fault of his own, is bullied and injured by someone who didn't even go to war!?" I pause and let the truth flow through.

I lock eyes with Aunt Jean. My eyes shift toward where Ted last stood. There's no white driving cap now. He's melted into the pavement. I pull back to my speech.

I tell the people that during the war years, Canada was like a semi-detached house. A row of semi-detached houses. People living close and concerned, listening through the walls and sharing, sharing, sharing scarce provisions and their sorrows.

"What Canada needs now is a way of sharing again. We don't need a war to remember how to share. What Canada needs are free doctors and hospitals. A way of protecting the forgotten, like Aunt Jean and Jimmy. Especially Jimmy, Aunt Jean's remaining son.

"One of the greatest Premiers in Canada, Tommy Douglas, says that the world cannot long survive half full and half hungry. He's right. And I say this Dominion of Canada can't go on if its people are half sick and half healthy. Because they can't afford to go to the doctor. Where's the freedom in that, Canada?"

I look up and see that Jimmy's in a bad way. He's been hemmed in too long, trying to be good. Aunt Jean looks pained. Andrew has Jimmy clamped in his arms. The crowd tries to move away from them.

"Jimmy. Jimmy, can you hear me? It's Carolyn."

I think it must have been God that did what came next, because it certainly wasn't me. I open my mouth and sing:

There'll be bluebirds over
The white cliffs of Dover
Tomorrow
Just you wait and see.

There'll be love and laughter
And peace ever after,
Tomorrow
When the world is free,

The shepherd will tend his sheep
The valleys will bloom again,
And Jimmy will go to sleep
In his own little room again,

My voice quivers when I mention Jimmy's name. I've
never before put two and two together that this is Jimmy's
song. Poor Jimmy, with no room for his sore head. The
second time I sing this verse, the choir begins to hum in
harmony. And then as one, they cut away and I sing the
last verse all by myself.

There'll be bluebirds over
The white cliffs of Dover,
Tomorrow
Just you wait and see.

"The White Cliffs of Dover!" Word perfect. Just as if the minister's song sheet was before me. When I finish, there isn't a sound except the wiffling of umbrellas.

"People like Aunt Jean and Jimmy need doctors. They need to see doctors for free so they can get on with their lives. So they don't end up on the street through no fault of their own. You can share, Canada, you can. You did it during the wars. You know that love is stronger than hate, kindness better than cruelty, and a helping hand more powerful than a clenched fist."

I raise my hand in the air and then let it fall to my side. I bow my head. Instead of *Amen* I say, "Lest We Forget" in the same tone.

Out of practice, I reach for my lace handkerchief and prepare to dab at my eyes. But now I'm dabbing at my eyes for real because I'm crying. God and Tommy Douglas together have exhausted me and I cling to the podium, looking in the direction of Jimmy and Aunt Jean.

Aunt Jean is smiling. No, beaming. She has her hands clasped to her heart.

The General salutes me.

My tears are so heavy now, that it's as if I'm swimming underwater with eyes open. One of my choir friends helps me to a seat. I don't remember the rest, except that I've just delivered a speech about why I am not, NOT proud to be Canadian. On Remembrance Day, no less.

Oh, my.

chapter

When we get home, Aunt Jean goes straight to her bed. And I go to mine, which is Andrew's now. He helps me off with my shoes and swings my legs up onto the bedspread. Then he tucks me in with an old quilt, I'm that shivery.

"It's just the adrenalin, is all. You'll be fine tomorrow. I'll fix you some hot honey and lemon."

Andrew shuts the door behind him. I can hear Jimmy on the floor snuffling around the crack worrying about me. Soon, he settles down, but he's still there on the floor blocking the hall light.

I never do get the drink Andrew promises me. "Out like a light, you were," he tells me the next day.

So out like a light that I sleep the whole night through

and miss my supper. I think it was the smell of bacon that woke my growling stomach. That, or the urgent need to use the toilet.

I peek out into the hallway. Aunt Jean's door is closed and Jimmy's too. If I hurry, I can be out of the house before she corners me to ask me questions.

I feel funny today. My grandpa would say that's what I get for wearing my heart on my sleeve.

I stop at the kitchen doorway, expecting to see Andrew or my mom at the stove, but the General's in charge.

"Goodness. I didn't expect to see you here."

"And good morning to you too, dear. Hot chocolate?"

"Yes, please. Where's Andrew?"

"I took his place on the couch. It looked to me like he needed a break from Jimmy-boy." The General pours straight from the saucepan into two mugs.

It's the most heavenly drink I ever tasted. I imagine chocolate syrup, thick and warm coursing like lava through my veins right to my toes. I close my eyes and feel the General watching me. He may have dealt with spies and prisoners of war, but he's no match for me. I'm not going to speak the first word about yesterday. Finally, the General clears his throat. "There's something I want

you to hear." He switches on CBC Radio and the eight
o'clock news.

There's a story about a fire, a bank robbery in London,
the weather's going to continue dark and drizzly, no
surprise there. And the Maple Leafs have beaten the
Canadiens. Finally, there's a special interest story. Aunt
Jean's kitchen is filled with sounds of the White Cliffs of
Dover. It takes me a minute to realize that it's me, ME
singing out of the radio. Then my speaking voice comes
on, not sounding like me at all. I'm reminding the whole
country of Canada, from sea to shining sea, to share. That
a country couldn't live half sick and half healthy.

"Gosh. Did I say that?" I can feel my eyes bugging right
out of their sockets.

A reporter sums up the words of "that little power-
house from Toronto who has lungs like Vera Lynn."

The General takes my cup from me and sets it down on
the table. Then he gathers me up in his arms and we polka
around the kitchen. "Yes you did. And more. You were
magnificent!" We hoot and holler and shriek ourselves
breathless. Such a carry-on, that neither of us spots Aunt
Jean watching us. I notice straight off the dark circles
under her eyes. They are red and swollen like she's been

crying all night long. The General lets go of me and wraps Aunt Jean in a big bear hug. "Carolyn's on the radio. She's famous, Jean. Wouldn't you know? A speech about why she's *not* proud to be Canadian makes her famous. But you're proud of her aren't you, Jean?"

"That I am." She reaches for me and pulls me close. "You should have told me sooner, Carolyn. You shouldn't have taken all that burden on your own shoulders."

Aunt Jean doesn't have to explain to me that we're talking about Ted now, and not Canada.

"Now, not another word until you've had breakfast." We don't argue with the General.

There's a mushroom omelet puffing in the iron frying pan and bacon warming and a basket of hot biscuits. Coffee for the General and Aunt Jean. Kid's tea for me. The more I eat, the more hungry I become. It's like I haven't eaten anything since Labor Day. When we are done, the General clears the table and we sit there facing each other.

"Now, Carolyn girl, do you have any questions for your aunt here?"

My mouth tries to form the words but no sound comes out. Finally I whisper. "Yes ... Yes, I do. ... Why is Ted so mean? Why does he hate you and Jimmy so much?"

Aunt Jean's shoulders begin to shake. She takes so long to answer that I think she never will.

"Ted's a . . . dirty rotten so-and-so because . . . he found out that . . ." A shudder goes through her, ". . . because he found out that he's not my brother at all."

"Then who is he? The bastard –" Goodness, Jimmy and I only put up with Ted for Aunt Jean's sake, because Ted was the only other relative she had.

"Now, now. There'll be none of that kind of language here," the General sputters.

"Then who the heck is he?"

"You're right, Carolyn, he is a bastard. He is a bastard . . . and I'm his mother."

"His mother! But you're Bertie's mother!"

"Yes. Bertie's *adopted* mother. Jake and I never thought we could have children because. . . . because, I had Ted so young, when I was fifteen years old. It messed me up in more ways than one." The General hands Aunt Jean a glass of tap water. She takes a long swallow.

"I ran with a wild crowd. I made a terrible mistake and my dad sent me away to 'private school' in Nova Scotia. My mother and I were pregnant at about the same time, and when she lost that baby, it seemed simple to switch hers with mine. There was no shame on this house and no one was the wiser. Until Ted tried to enlist. . . . He ordered up his birth certificate."

The General reaches for Aunt Jean's hand to give her courage, but she pulls away. She looks shriveled and alone.

"Ted was so upset when he found out. And who can blame him? Then Bertie died, and so much fuss was made about our son, who Ted said wasn't even a blood relative. And then we had our miracle baby. Jimmy."

Aunt Jean's face softens when she mentions Jimmy's name and then tenses up again. "Ted let it eat at him. That, and being turned down for the service because of his flat feet."

"*Oh-h-h-h-h.* I see." And I did see. Poor Ted. A bastard for real. And me an almost bastard. It was like Ted's whole life was a story on a blackboard and with one swipe of a wet chamois, was wiped right out. You had to start again and think about things differently from the very beginning. And it's no wonder that Bertie missed having the blessed flat feet. No wonder at all. It makes sense now.

"I'm sorry, honey. I've been willfully blind about Ted. I've been consumed by remorse and regret and responsibility. I was so relieved when he seemed to do so well financially. When your mom wouldn't let him take over the house, properly mind, he saw red. He thought it was his chance to be the head of the household. To take his rightful place. And steal me blind in the process. I blame myself. But I've done making excuses for poor Ted." Aunt Jean takes another shaky sip of water.

"I'm done with Ted. This family is done with him. There are some things that can't be undone. Lord knows, I've tried."

I look up at the General. "Is she still going to lose the house?"

"I'll answer that! It is immaterial to me whether or not I lose this house. This house is just bricks and mortar. Bricks and mortar. Nothing at all compared to the health of my Jimmy ... and the safety of you, Carolyn. Nothing at all. We'll get along. We always do."

We let that hang there for about ten seconds. Finally, the General clears his throat. "Now, Jean. Is there something you'd like to ask Carolyn?"

I tell the whole story about how Jimmy flew out the back of Ted's car. I don't intend to ever tell it again, but I must say that I was wrong about half-believing the swing story. The true details hit me right in the heart. All over again.

Poor Jimmy. Poor Aunt Jean. Poor, poor Ted.

I look up when I've finished the story. My mom is leaning against the doorjamb. She, too, is in her pajamas and her robe and she's gripping a coffee mug so tightly, I think it will shatter. Her face is white, her lips bloodless. The cords of her neck are sticking out and I see a pulse beating where her throat meets her neck. The look on her face is the same one she had when I was in Grade 2 and Luanne Price called me a poor little bastard.

"Carolyn, that night . . . the night when you stayed at the MacGregor's . . . the night that Jimmy was sick –"

"Drunk," interrupts Aunt Jean. "The night that Ted got Jimmy drunk. From here in, we must speak the plain truth of it."

"All right then, the night that Ted got Jimmy drunk. Did Ted hurt you? Did he put his hands on you?"

I know what she means. Did Ted attack me? Did he violate me because I'm a girl? I tug at the sleeve of my pajama top, pulling it down over the wrist that Ted grabbed as he pulled me to him. The bruises have long since disappeared, but not the memory of his strength. The gasoline smell of his breath on my face. The rasp of his whiskers. No. These memories have not gone away.

I look at Aunt Jean's face. Her eyelids are fluttering and I think she's praying to the Lord that nothing bad has happened to me. She looks desperate to know if Ted has sunk to new depths.

Suddenly, I'm very calm. While I understand that there are things about Jimmy that need to be told, there are things about me and Ted, which Mom and Aunt Jean do *not* need to know. What would be the point? I'll get over Ted's demands that I give him a kiss. His drunken leering at me from top to toe, in that way.

I look up at the General. He mouths the word *later* and I seize on it like a life ring.

I will tell the General.

"No," I whisper. "He never harmed me. He could never catch me to hurt me. I'm small, but I'm fast." I laugh like I've just told the funniest joke. Mom and Aunt Jean laugh with me, so anxious to believe that I'm telling the truth. The General gives me a nod. He's not so easily fooled. He ruffles my hair and makes room for my mother at the table.

"More tea?" he says to me.

"Yes, please." And so, I turn the page on Ted.

chapter

22

I don't go to school. I stay in my pajamas all day and we play Scrabble and Crokinole and drink mint tea like we all have bellyaches instead of heartaches.

So it isn't until two days later that I face the class after my Remembrance Day speech. Not a pencil shaving drops when I enter the classroom. The hair climbs straight up on my arms, the atmosphere is that spooky.

And then they cheer. All the kids cheer except the horrid Luanne Price who stares an ugly stare at me, through my forehead and all the way to the back cloakroom. It seems I was not only on the CBC Radio, but on CBC Television too. I have to say that it never occurred to me that our local Remembrance Day ceremony would be televised. You see, Aunt Jean doesn't have a television and neither do we. But everybody else seems to. Pity I never saw it.

Mostly, because of that television broadcast, mail starts pouring in. Letters for Aunt Jean, some of them with cheques enclosed.

I've been getting mail, too, although its beginning to dwindle. Mostly I get letters from classrooms of kids whose teachers have obviously made them write me. Sometimes I get a group letter containing one line from each kid about why they are proud to be Canadian. I feel bad about that because it was never my intention to make my speech homework. I have about five letters from choirmasters asking me if I want a new job. There are six letters from little girls asking for advice on how they can become actresses and go on the CBC.

But the best letter of all is a stiff and heavy envelope with an embossed coat of arms of Saskatchewan on the flap. I know who this is from and I hug it to my chest.

"Well, open it!" says Aunt Jean.

Jimmy bellows his support. I take a knife from the drawer and carefully slit open the package. Inside, there's a signed picture of Tommy C. Douglas. And there's a hand-written note.

"What's he say? What's he say?"

I read it right through to the end and start again. I fold it up and put it back in the envelope.

"Well?"

"He likes me."

"Of course, he likes you. We all like you. Land sakes. Such a girl, Jimmy."

The letter from Tommy Douglas is my treasure. I'm not sharing. Except maybe with Jimmy when he goes to bed. He'll like the story about how Tommy Douglas hurt his leg and had a bone infection and was going to lose his leg until a doctor stepped up and said he would operate on it for free.

It's a sign.

With the money and the publicity, a miracle has happened. A lawyer has come forward (I suspect he's a friend of the General) and determined that Uncle Ted's mortgage is a flimflam. A fraud. It's not properly signed. There's no evidence that Aunt Jean's husband borrowed anything from Ted. I guess Ted was trying to take what he thought he was rightfully owed. The General says Ted's lucky that he didn't get his tail landed in jail.

Oh yes, and Aunt Jean has been given a little job through Veterans Affairs that she can do right here at home.

But best of all, the Bank of Nova Scotia has opened up a fund for Jimmy's operation. Money is pouring in from across the country. Soon there should be enough money to pay Dr. Phillips at Sick Children's Hospital.

As I told you, our Jimmy is not a mental defective like Luanne Price says. Our Jimmy is in there. He's in there. This I know. And Dr. Phillips will let him out.

And as for Ted? I admit that there's never been a Thursday yet that he doesn't cross my mind. But he's long gone. And if he shows up again? Never mind. We can deal with Ted. As I said at the beginning, he doesn't scare me. Never has. Never will.

I'm not afraid of anything.

Not anymore.